A Stallion Called Midnight

Victoria Eveleigh

Illustrated by Chris Eveleigh

Orion
Children's Books

First published in Great Britain under the
title *Midnight on Lundy* in 2009
by Tortoise Publishing
This edition first published in 2012
by Orion Children's Books
a division of the Orion Publishing Group Ltd
Orion House
5 Upper St Martin's Lane
London WC2H 9EA
An Hachette UK Company

1 3 5 7 9 10 8 6 4 2

Text copyright © Victoria Eveleigh 2009, 2012
Illustrations copyright © Chris Eveleigh 2009, 2012

The right of Victoria Eveleigh and Chris Eveleigh
to be identified as the author and illustrator
of this work has been asserted.

The Orion Publishing Group's policy is to use papers
that are natural, renewable and recyclable products and
made from wood grown in sustainable forests. The logging
and manufacturing processes are expected to conform to
the environmental regulations of the country of origin.

A catalogue record for this book is
available from the British Library.

Printed in Great Britain by Clays Ltd, St Ives plc

ISBN 978 1 4440 0552 3

www.orionbooks.co.uk

For Diana.
Thank you for all your help
and for some wonderful holidays on Lundy.

Lundy

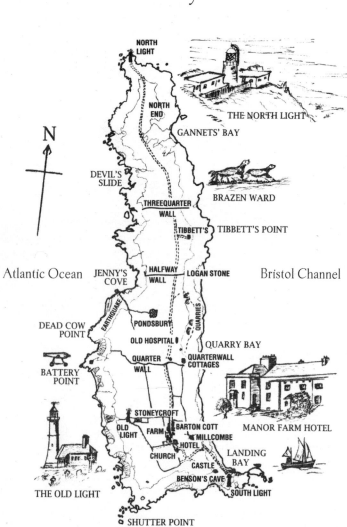

NORTH LIGHT

THE NORTH LIGHT

NORTH END

GANNETS' BAY

N

DEVIL'S SLIDE

BRAZEN WARD

THREEQUARTER WALL

TIBBETT'S   TIBBETT'S POINT

Atlantic Ocean   JENNY'S COVE   HALFWAY WALL   LOGAN STONE   Bristol Channel

EARTHQUAKE

DEAD COW POINT   PONDSBURY   QUARRIES

OLD HOSPITAL   QUARRY BAY

BATTERY POINT   QUARTER WALL   QUARTERWALL COTTAGES

STONEYCROFT

OLD LIGHT   FARM   BARTON COTT   MANOR FARM HOTEL

MILLCOMBE

HOTEL

CHURCH   LANDING BAY

CASTLE

BENSON'S CAVE

THE OLD LIGHT   SOUTH LIGHT

SHUTTER POINT

PART I

An Island Kingdom

1

Jenny fled up the stony track from the village. "I won't go! *I won't!*" she shouted.

The wind snatched her words and carried them over the sea towards the mainland – towards that other world which had played little part in her life, until now.

"I'm perfectly happy living with Dad," she said to herself, "and I've got plenty of friends. There are the islanders, lighthouse-keepers, fishermen, summer workers, visitors; you can't have many more friends than that! So why does Dad think I need to make friends and learn about the world? Why will it be *good* for me to go away to that stupid school?"

"Stupid, stupid school" Jenny screamed into the wind.

She struggled to shut the gate at Quarter Wall. Then she turned and ran, with the wind chasing her, towards the quarries.

What if nobody likes me? she worried. What if I don't like them? It'll be like going to prison. Miles from Lundy, miles from Dad and, worst of all, miles from Midnight.

Jenny couldn't remember life without Midnight. He'd been the herd stallion since before she was born. He was the king, and Lundy was his kingdom. He roamed where he liked, jumping the walls with ease, and he took orders from nobody. Everyone who had tried to catch and tame him had failed miserably. Everyone except Jenny – but that was their secret.

Jenny picked her way down the slippery path to the old quarries, knowing where she'd choose to shelter from a south-westerly gale if she were a pony.

She was right. The ponies were in the second quarry, protected from the elements by the massive walls which made a kind of open cave looking out to sea. It was a peaceful sanctuary, while the storm raged all around and waves crashed against the rocks below.

Three foals had been born so far. Jenny sat down on a slab of granite, and watched as they played together. She loved their ruffled, fluffy coats. Two foals were a creamy colour with pale grey legs. They'd probably end up golden dun with black points, like Midnight.

The third was a light roan. Foals had to be the best baby animals in the world.

The mares dozed or wandered around picking at the plants that grew between the stones. They took no notice of the small, slender girl in their midst.

Jenny had spent so much time with the ponies that they probably thought she was another feral animal – once domesticated but now wild, like them. She liked the idea. Mrs Hamilton was always calling her a wild child.

"Why, oh *why*?" Jenny cried out, startling a couple of mares nearby. "Oops, sorry!" she said, lowering her voice. "I mean, why does anything have to change? Why can't Mrs Hamilton carry on teaching me? She must have done a pretty good job so far, or I wouldn't have got that scholarship, would I? And why was I told that exam was just a test to see how well I was doing?"

She gazed at the idyllic scene before her, and sighed. "I can't go away! I *can't!*" she said.

As if in agreement, Midnight walked up and nuzzled her short brown hair.

Jenny looked into his extraordinary midnight-blue eyes. "I wish I was a pony, Midnight. Life's simple for you, isn't it? You don't have to worry about exams and schools, or being sent to the mainland. All you have to do is find water, food and shelter."

Midnight gave a snort.

Jenny's cold fingers snuggled into the warm, soft

hair under his thick mane. "Okay, so you have to take care of the mares and foals, I suppose, but that's not a hard job, is it? They pretty well take care of themselves, leaving you plenty of time to do as you please." She stood up on the granite slab and leaned over Midnight's broad back.

He shifted his weight slightly, but didn't move away.

Without a second thought, Jenny leapt lightly onto him, and sat there as if it were the most natural thing in the world. It didn't even occur to her that riding a wild stallion without a saddle or bridle was dangerous.

He wandered along the old quarry terrace, nibbling at the sparse vegetation. Jenny just sat there and talked about anything and everything.

Midnight and Jenny seemed to have an understanding; he allowed her to sit on his back, and she let him do as he pleased – mainly because she didn't know how to get him to do anything else.

"I wish I could ride properly," Jenny told him. "Then we could gallop over the island, jumping everything in our way. Wouldn't that be fun?"

Riding lessons were the one thing Jenny longed for which she couldn't get on Lundy. Nobody else on the island seemed particularly interested in the ponies, beyond the fact they were nice to look at and had become a traditional part of Lundy – almost as popular as puffins with the tourists.

If only Mum . . . Jenny began to think, and then stopped herself. Dad said "if onlys" could drive you mad, and he was right.

By the time they got back to the quarry, Jenny's jeans were cold and clammy from Midnight's damp coat. They clung uncomfortably, chilling her body to shivering point.

"Time to go home and face the music," she said, giving Midnight a farewell rub on his shoulder. His lips quivered in ecstasy, and his eyes started to close.

"You big baby!" she teased. "It's lucky nobody else knows what a softy you are. Promise me you'll stay wild with everyone else, won't you? You'll stay safe and free as long as you're wild."

Midnight nudged Jenny with his nose. "Good boy," she said, scratching him under his chin. "Now, I really must be going."

Although Jenny was cold she ambled home reluctantly, taking the longer route through the north entrance to the quarries. The wind had calmed to a fresh breeze and a watery sun, like a torch with flat batteries, hung low in the sky. She hadn't realised how late it was.

As she walked past the farm buildings she saw her dad, Robert Medway, walking towards her with his long, easy stride. There was no escape; she'd have to talk to him.

"Thank goodness you're back. I was beginning to worry," he said. "I've just fed your animals for you. Do you want to help me with the chickens?"

She scuffed some gravel with her foot. "Okay."

"I'll get the corn, and you can collect the eggs," he said.

Jenny never tired of egg-collecting; it was like hunting for treasure. She went to the back of the wooden chicken shed, and opened the flap covering the nesting boxes.

The rusty hinges creaked.

She felt inside, her fingers searching for smooth eggs nestling in the straw. Instead, they dipped into the slimy contents of a jagged eggshell. As she withdrew her fingers something furry writhed against them. She snatched her hand away and peered cautiously into the long, dark box.

A large rat glared back, whiskers twitching, surrounded by a gooey mess of broken eggshells. It leapt out of the box and ran for cover under the shed.

Jenny screamed and jumped back, dropping the flap with a bang.

Dad hurried over, corn spilling from the feed scoop in his hand. "What's happened? Are you all right?"

"A rat! A really big one! Under there!" she squeaked.

"All the eggs are broken! Ruined!"

Dad swore. "They've been in the vegetable garden too; it's a never-ending battle. Poor old you!" He hugged his daughter, holding her close.

Jenny loved his hugs. They were safe and solid.

"Ah well, rabbit stew for supper tonight," Dad said.

All the tensions of the day welled up and exploded inside Jenny, like a wave crashing against rocks. She burst into tears.

"Hey, what's up?"

"Everything! I hate rats and I hate rabbit stew!" she wailed into her father's coat.

He stroked her damp hair. "I bet they don't eat rabbit stew at St Anne's."

Oh no! Jenny thought. Here comes the lecture.

Dad hugged her tightly, engulfing her thin body in his strong arms. "I'm so proud of you," he said. "A scholarship to St Anne's really is a great achievement, you know."

"But I don't want to go, Dad! I know I'll hate it there!" She glanced up at him. "And why didn't you tell me it was a scholarship exam? Why did you lie?"

"Oh, Jenny! I thought you'd love to go away to school and be with girls your own age for a change, rather than being stuck here the whole time. I couldn't afford to send you without the money for the scholarship, but I didn't want you to feel under pressure or to be disappointed if you failed. It was a white lie, I suppose."

"What's a white lie?"

"A lie told to avoid hurting someone's feelings."

"Oh. Well, it didn't work, did it?" Jenny looked up again, and met her father's concerned gaze. "This is my home. I love it here. Why does anything have to change? Please don't make me go!"

"Of course I won't *make* you go, Jenny, but you'll be missing the greatest opportunity of your life – and a lot of fun, too." Dad lowered his voice to a secret whisper. "I've heard there are stables nearby, and riding's an optional extra. You'd be able to have lessons every week. Would you like that?"

Riding lessons! Jenny thought. Perhaps if she went away to school for a little while – just a term or two – she could learn to ride and then come home again for good. Riding lessons cost a lot of money, though. And she'd need riding clothes, like the girls in the *Princess Pony Annual* Mrs Hamilton had given her for Christmas. It would all be hopelessly expensive.

"Would you like riding lessons?" Dad asked again.

"Of course I would, but we can't afford it," she answered. "Also, I'll need boots, a hat, jodhpurs, a jacket and a yellow polo neck." She'd always longed for a yellow polo neck. She imagined herself looking like the girl on the front cover of the annual.

"I expect we'll manage somehow. Summer's coming

up, so you'll be able to earn some money in the Hotel, and I'll get all the extra jobs I can. If you want riding lessons, you shall have them."

Jenny couldn't help smiling now. "Do you mean it?"

Dad smiled back. "Of course I mean it."

"I suppose school *could* be okay, if there's riding as well."

"I bet it'll be more than okay. It'll be great fun, you wait and see." Dad put his arm round Jenny's shoulder and turned towards home. "Meg! That'll do!" he called to his sheepdog as she tried, in vain, to get at the rat under the chicken shed.

A new world of possibilities opened up to Jenny. "Perhaps I could keep my own pony at the stables," she said, secretly thinking of Midnight.

Dad laughed and ruffled her hair. "Don't push your luck, young lady!"

Ah well, it was worth a try.

2

Typical, Jenny thought as she made sandwiches in the Hotel kitchen. It's the first day that really feels like summer, and the place is buzzing with visitors. Still, they'll be gone by four-thirty, so there'll be time for a swim before I go to see the ponies.

On boat days hundreds of people came by steamer to visit Lundy, and they all had to be fed and looked after. Boat days were hard work for everyone, but they brought much-needed money to the island.

Jenny spread butter on slices of bread, put in the fillings, cut the sandwiches and stacked them on a tray. Her hands made sandwiches, but her mind thought ponies. Kittiwake, the youngest mare, would be having her first foal soon. Kit was quite tame, probably because she'd become so used to Jenny. She was a beautiful pony, with four white socks and a white star, and her body was a mottled grey-brown colour, like granite. Her foal was bound to be gorgeous.

"There you are, Jenny!" Mrs Hamilton stood at the kitchen door. "There's someone I want you to meet. She's your age, and she's pony-mad, just like you! You'd love to spend some time with her and show her the sights, wouldn't you? Don't worry about helping me in the Tea Garden this afternoon, I'll manage."

"Um . . ."

"Splendid! Here we are, then. Isabella, this is Jenny Medway, our farm manager's daughter. Jenny, this is Isabella Wagstaff."

Jenny was sure Mrs Hamilton had got Isabella's age wrong. She looked at least sixteen, with her skimpy navy blue shorts and matching blue striped T-shirt. Her arms and legs were long, slim and sun-tanned, and her silky dark hair was tied back with a navy blue ribbon. Usually Jenny didn't care what she looked like, but at that moment she felt terribly small and self-conscious in her baggy hand-me-down khaki shorts and faded yellow shirt.

"Well, I can see you two are going to get along famously, so I'll leave you to your adventures!" said Mrs Hamilton. "I must get on. Remember, the boat leaves at four-thirty. Have fun!" The click-clack of her shoes faded as she marched away down the corridor.

Isabella and Jenny stood staring at each other, as if they were from different planets.

Sheila, the cook, broke the silence. "You get going, Jenny. I'll finish up here. Take a couple of sandwiches, if you like."

Sheila was short, plump and Scottish. She had curly red hair and the sort of freckled skin which never tanned, even in mid-summer. Mr Hamilton called her "a good sort".

"Thanks, Sheila. Is a cheese sandwich okay for you, Isabella?" asked Jenny.

"Fine," Isabella said, without enthusiasm.

Usually Jenny enjoyed showing visitors the island, but she felt like a fish out of water with Isabella. Still, taking her sightseeing had to be better than making sandwiches.

"Where would you like to go?" she asked as they walked out into the bright sunshine.

"I don't know. You're the guide," Isabella replied.

"Okay. How about starting with the Church, as we're so close to it?"

Isabella sighed. "If we *must*. Isn't there anything more exciting to see?"

"How about the Castle? It's not far, and there's a

lovely view from there. We'll be able to see the steamer in the Landing Bay."

Jenny tried to make conversation by telling Isabella about places of interest along the way, but she didn't seem at all interested. They lapsed into an awkward silence.

As they reached the Castle, Isabella said, "Doesn't look much like a castle to me. More like a badly built house with no windows."

"It's the oldest building on Lundy. It's got tons of history," Jenny said, ready with tales of the Mariscos, Thomas Benson and dastardly deeds.

"I'll take your word for it," Isabella replied.

"Let's go down to Benson's Cave. There's a great view from there." Jenny led the way down the steep bank to the cave.

Isabella slipped on the grass in her deck shoes, and ended up inching down cautiously on her bottom, glancing nervously at the sheer drop to her right. "This had better be worth it," she said, dusting herself off. She peered through the narrow entrance to Benson's Cave, and wrinkled her nose. "Is this little hole supposed to be a cave?"

"I know it doesn't look much, but it's quite large inside. It was used for storing smuggled goods," Jenny said.

"Wow-ee!" Isabella mocked.

When all else fails, eat, Jenny thought, sitting down

on a grassy ledge near the cave. She handed a couple of sandwiches to Isabella, who took them without a word of thanks.

After nibbling a bit from the centre, Isabella threw most of her sandwich over the cliff. Before long a couple of gulls found the easy meal. Then others swooped in. Soon a riot of gulls squabbled beneath them. Fascinated, Isabella tore up her second sandwich and tossed it down to them, bit by bit.

Jenny was shocked. Food was never wasted or taken for granted on Lundy.

While Isabella fed the gulls, Jenny ate her sandwiches. The sun shone from a cloudless sky, picking out every detail of the breathtaking scenery around them. Boats of various sizes speckled the bright blue sea and clustered round the steamer in the bay to the left. Ahead, a rocky peninsula rose up like a monster from the deep, topped by the gleaming white bulk of the South Light.

This must be the most beautiful place on earth, Jenny thought.

"I pity the poor person who has to live there," said Isabella, pointing at the lighthouse.

"Albert lives there – Albert Scoines. He's the PK. He says it's the best job in the world."

"What on earth's a PK?"

"Principal Keeper. You see, the lighthouses on

14

Lundy are rock lights, so there are three resident keepers in each. The keepers live there together, while their families live on the mainland. They do two months on duty, and then have a month's leave ashore. The PK is the head man in each light."

"Fascinating," Isabella murmured. She was lying on the grass with her eyes closed.

Jenny wasn't good at spotting sarcasm. "The PK of the North Light is Gareth. He's okay, but he sometimes gets a bit moody after a few beers. Albert is definitely the nicest keeper. In fact, he's the nicest person I know – apart from Dad, of course."

Isabella's eyes remained closed. "What about your mother?"

Jenny froze. All the islanders knew what had happened to Mum, so she'd never had to tell anyone before.

The gulls stopped squawking. The cliffs fell silent, as if holding their breath, willing Jenny to reply.

"She died when I was five." There, she'd said it.

Isabella looked embarrassed. She sat up and picked at the grass by her side. Then she said brightly, "Oh well, mothers are pretty useless, really. Daddy always says Mummy's main function in life is to spend money as fast as he can make it."

Jenny stared at her, speechless. There was an uncomfortable silence.

Isabella quickly changed the subject. "I love going

15

abroad, don't you?" she said. "Properly abroad, I mean, like the Mediterranean."

Jenny gave up trying to be polite. "Why did you come here, then?"

With a disarming smile, Isabella said, "Daddy's a financial advisor. He's come here on some sort of business, so I thought it would be fun to come too. He's got an important meeting with the owner, Mr Bonham, and someone called, er, Donald Hamilton?"

"Mr Hamilton's the agent. He lives here."

"Oh, I see. That would explain why Daddy's meeting him. Anyway, this is just a day trip. We're all going to America for a proper family holiday in August. Where do you go for your summer holidays?"

Before she could stop herself Jenny said, "Corfu." It was the first place which sprang to mind.

"Really? Isn't Corfu great? We went there last year!" Isabella exclaimed. "Did you go to the Canal D'Amour?"

"Oh yes, we went all over the place," Jenny replied. What on earth was she playing at? An occasional trip to the mainland was her idea of going abroad. "So you like ponies, do you?" she asked, in a desperate attempt to change the subject.

"Of course I like ponies! We've got several at home, but my favourite is Dinglefoot Creation. Her stable name is Creo. Daddy bought her for me last year, for an awful lot of money, and already I've won so

16

many rosettes that there's no room for them all on my bedroom door. I just keep the firsts and throw away the rest. Daddy always says that if you don't compete to win, there's no point."

Jenny had homemade paper rosettes stuck onto her bedroom door, from pretend horse shows with cut-out paper ponies. A real rosette of any colour would have been a treasured possession.

"What's your pony called?" Isabella asked. It was clear that in her world everyone had a pony or two.

"Midnight," Jenny said, without a moment's hesitation. Lying was surprisingly easy.

"Black, I bet," said Isabella.

"No. A sort of golden colour, with a dark mane and tail, and dark blue eyes."

"That's unusual. Is Midnight a mare or a gelding?"

"Actually, he's a stallion."

"Wow! You don't ride him, do you?"

Jenny revelled in Isabella's look of admiration. "Yes," she said. Why had she said that? She'd given away her greatest secret to a stranger she didn't like, just to impress her. *Why? Why? Why?*

"Wow!" Isabella said again. "Is he good at jumping?"

"Oh yes, excellent. He's jumped over pretty well every wall on the island." Well, there was no harm in telling her that, was there? Everyone knew he was good at jumping.

"That's amazing!" Isabella exclaimed. "Some of those walls are really high!" She seemed totally lost for words as they climbed back up the slope to the Castle. When they reached the top she said, "Can I ride him?"

Jenny had to think fast. "I'm afraid not. He's running out with the mares just now, and the herd could be anywhere," she said, trying to sound genuinely sorry. "Would you like to see some puffins, though? There's a colony at the Battery. It isn't too far away." She prayed Midnight hadn't jumped the wall into Ackland's Moor, which he sometimes did for fun.

The girls didn't have any binoculars, and most of the puffins were sheltering in their burrows, but they saw a few.

By the time they got back to the village they were tired and dizzy from the strong sun. Mrs Hamilton was serving teas, so they stopped for a quick drink and some biscuits. Her main job was managing the Manor Farm Hotel but, like all the islanders, she turned her hand to anything that needed doing. Hotel guests were sometimes amazed to see the immaculate Mrs Hamilton sorting sheep or setting seed potatoes ready for the plough to turn in.

As they walked down the Beach Road Isabella said,

"Thanks for showing me around. I'm sorry we didn't see Midnight, but I must admit I've enjoyed today more than I thought I would."

"Thanks for getting me out of working in the kitchens all day," Jenny replied. She felt absurdly pleased that Isabella now seemed to like her.

When they reached the Landing Beach, it was a hive of activity. A couple of boats transported small groups of visitors from a tractor-pulled landing stage to the steamer. This involved a lot of effort, and most of the islanders were helping in some way.

Isabella scanned the crowd expectantly. "Daddy!" she shouted.

Several people turned round to look. A large, powerfully built man dressed in a suit stood a short distance from the main crowd on the beach. He ground his cigarette into the shingle, pointed to the landing stage and started walking purposefully towards it.

"Looks like I'd better go. Good luck with the jumping," said Isabella. "Perhaps I'll see you at a show sometime." Then she hurried to join her father.

Jenny watched the Wagstaffs make their way to the landing stage. The people in the queue let them go to the front without question. Mr Wagstaff looked as if he owned the place.

The real owner, Mr Bonham, blended in with the islanders in his shorts and open-necked shirt as he helped people aboard and wished them a safe journey.

I didn't really lie, Jenny told herself. Midnight's practically mine, anyway. I just told a few white lies which made Isabella much friendlier. Besides, we'll never see each other again, so no harm's done.

3

Jenny woke early. The rising summer sun shone like a spotlight on her bed. She lay still for a while, listening to the sound of her bedroom curtains shifting in the gentle breeze. Faraway noises wafted in – gulls, birds, farm animals – and she savoured the wonderful feeling that a perfect day lay ahead. No day-visitors and no work, just beautiful weather and the whole island to explore. What could be better? She got up, tiptoed into the kitchen, quietly gathered together some food and left a note saying she'd be back in time for supper. Then she slipped out of the house before her dad woke up and found her a job.

Once outside, Jenny went over to the farmyard to

feed her pet animals: six chickens, a tame goat called Ermintrude – who was due to give birth soon – and two orphan lambs called Dot and Dash. The lambs had been adorable when they'd been babies struggling for survival, but they weren't adorable any more. Since March they'd grown into noisy, demanding little thugs who frequently knocked her over in their rush to get at the milk bottle. Feeding them was now a chore rather than a pleasure, as her father had warned her it would be when she'd begged him to let her keep them. Her determination to prove him wrong was the main thing which kept her feeding them religiously twice a day.

As soon as she'd seen to her animals, Jenny hurried away to find the ponies. They were by the Old Hospital ruins, lazing in the morning sun. Kit still hadn't foaled. She looked as round as a barrel, standing nose-to-tail with her best friend, Dunlin. The foals lay flat out while their mothers stood over them, heavy-eyed and droopy-lipped. A few drowsy insects buzzed between the wildflowers, waiting for the day to begin in earnest. The grass glistened with dewdrops. Seabirds called in the distance.

Rosie, the oldest pony in the herd, who seemed to be the lead mare, stood next to Midnight. They were always together. Rosie was strawberry roan, with no white markings at all.

Midnight stirred as Jenny approached. He raised his

head, and his nostrils flickered in recognition.

"Hello, handsome," she said, stroking his shoulder. "Guess what? I dreamed I owned you last night, and we entered a show-jumping competition and beat Isabella! We got a great big red rosette, and she chucked away her blue one."

Midnight lowered his head and relaxed while she talked to him and rubbed his sleek summer coat, working in small circles down his neck and along his back. He always went into a sleepy trance when she did that, with a blissful look on his face.

"Perhaps one day I really will own you. Would you like that?" Jenny said. "Actually, I suppose you don't realise you're owned by *anyone*. It's such a weird idea, isn't it? I mean, what gives us the right to own things and decide what happens to them? Horses, dogs, farm animals, land – whole islands, even."

Midnight blew gently through his nose, and rested a hind leg.

"If horses *do* think they own things, I bet you reckon this place belongs to you," Jenny said. Her arm began to ache. She stopped rubbing Midnight, and walked back to the track so she could sit on a stone.

He followed, as if she were leading him.

She started running, to see what would happen, and he trotted after her. She ran in circles, trying to catch him out, but he followed like a shadow, stopping when she stopped and tagging along when she moved. Magic!

Looking up, Jenny caught sight of two people walking along the track towards them.

"Shoo! Shoo!" she hissed, waving her arms and jumping up and down. She couldn't let anyone see Midnight being so tame.

Alarmed by her sudden madness, Midnight shied away, kicking up his heels, and dashed back to the mares and foals.

The taller person ran towards her. As he came nearer, she realised it was Albert. "Are you all right, Jenny?" he called. "You're not hurt, are you?"

For a moment she couldn't understand what he was talking about, but then she realised it must have looked as if Midnight was chasing her. "Yes, I'm fine, thanks. I think I must have got a bit close," she answered.

Albert reached her. "Thank goodness for that," he said. "You really shouldn't get too near the ponies, you know. Mares with foals can be dangerous, and that stallion's a devil." He turned to the teenage boy behind him. "Jenny, this is my son, Ben. He came over on the boat yesterday. He's working here for the summer, but Mr Hamilton's given him the day off, so he can get to know the place."

Ben had his father's bright blue eyes and friendly smile, but otherwise Jenny wouldn't have known they were related. Albert was tall and slim, with a full head of well-cut silvery hair. Ben had floppy fair hair and a stocky, solid body. Like a well-built pony, Jenny thought approvingly. She guessed he was about sixteen years old.

"Do you always get up this early?" Ben asked.

"Sometimes. I wanted to see if Kit had foaled, but she hasn't," Jenny replied. "What about you?"

"Dad's on watch after dinner, so I had to get up early for a grand tour of the island."

"We're heading to the North Light for some breakfast," said Albert. "Do you want to come?"

"Yes, please!" Jenny said. The day was turning out even better than expected.

Grit crunched beneath their feet as they walked along the track to the North Light. Albert strode on ahead, occasionally stopping to watch birds through his binoculars, leaving Jenny and Ben to talk.

"Have schools on the mainland broken up for the summer holidays already?" Jenny asked.

"Not really," Ben replied. "But I left last week, as soon as I could. No more school for me, thank goodness. What about you? Is there a school on Lundy?"

"Sort of, I suppose, but I'm the only pupil. I'm taught by Mrs Hamilton. She runs the Hotel."

"I think I've met her. Large, efficient and scary?"

"That's the one," Jenny giggled. "Once she made me rinse my mouth out with soap and water for swearing."

"You're joking!" exclaimed Ben.

"She's not that bad, really. She's very strict, but pretty fair, and she works awfully hard. Dad says the island would grind to a halt without her. She's a good teacher, too. I got a scholarship to St Anne's because of her." Jenny felt her insides lurch, as they did whenever she allowed herself to think about her new school.

"What, the poshest school in North Devon?"

Jenny felt herself blushing. "I suppose so, unless there are two called St Anne's."

"Crikey! What are you hoping to be? A brain surgeon?"

It had never occurred to Jenny that she would have to *be* anything. As far as she was concerned, she'd go to school, learn how to ride and then live on Lundy forever. She'd probably run the Stores or something. "I haven't really given it much thought," she said. "Definitely not a brain surgeon, though. Ugh! What about you? What are you going to be?"

"A farmer. A farmer with a boat, though. I could never be far from the sea."

"Just like Dad! Perhaps you'll have to take over his job here when he retires, although that won't be for ages. He says he could never live anywhere else. I suppose everyone who lives here feels like that."

"How many people live here, then, apart from the lighthouse-keepers?"

Jenny counted on her fingers. "There's me, Dad, Mr and Mrs Hamilton . . . Twelve all year-round, I think, or seventeen if you count the Bonhams. Then from Easter onwards, lots more people come and go: Mr Bonham's brother and his family, other guests at Millcombe, Field Society members, visitors in the Hotel and the cottages, fishermen and sailors, seasonal workers – all sorts."

"Nice to know I'm an *all sorts.*"

"Well, it's better than being a bluebottle."

"What's a bluebottle?"

"A day-tripper. They come in like a swarm of flies, buzz around for a bit and then buzz off." Jenny gave a demonstration, buzzing up the track.

Ben followed, laughing, and they caught up with Albert.

"The wildlife's up early this morning," he said in a low voice.

Jenny immediately saw what he meant, and giggled. "Here comes Batty," she whispered to Ben.

A large, grey-haired gentleman with a bushy white beard marched along the track towards them. Despite the promise of a hot day, he wore a thick tweed jacket, a shirt and tie, plus-fours, long green socks and walking boots. A huge pair of binoculars hung round his neck.

"What-ho, Jenny! Morning, Albert! We're all up at sparrow's fart this morning, by the looks of it!"

Jenny caught Ben's eye, and they both snorted with suppressed laughter.

"Good morning, Major Bathurst. May I introduce my son, Ben? He's working here for a few weeks. Ben, this is Major Bathurst, who lives at Tibbett's – the old Admiralty lookout over there."

"What-ho, Ben! Welcome to the madhouse!" Batty roared, and he carried on towards the village.

On Tibbett's Hill, the whole of the north end of Lundy opened up before them, like the deck of a vast ship.

As they walked on, the tussocky grass gradually gave way to granite outcrops encrusted with dry heather and lichens. A fire years ago had destroyed most of the peaty soil, and the land was taking a long time to recover. It was bleak and wild. Jenny loved it.

They were talking so much that it seemed no time at all before they were through the North Light's narrow entrance between the rocks, and descending the long cascade of steps down to the lighthouse.

Albert knocked on the pristine door of the North Light, then walked in before it was answered.

"Come in! No need to knock!" a voice shouted from a room at the end of the white corridor.

The lighthouses were another world; a ship-shape, impersonal world of paint, shiny brass and squeaky-clean glass.

"You couldn't have come at a better moment, the kettle's just boiled," Gareth said as he took a blue enamel kettle off the cooker. Its ear-splitting whistle subsided to a soft whine. He handed round heavy mugs of tea, and put a bowl of sugar lumps and a jug of condensed milk on the table. Then he went along to the foot of the stone stairs. "Cup of tea, John?" he shouted. "John's on duty at the moment, and Neil's having a kip," he explained on his return.

"No I'm not. I heard the kettle. Got visitors? Wow, a party!" Neil said, yawning and rubbing his eyes as he walked into the kitchen, followed by John.

"Good to see you, Neil. How's life, John?" Albert asked.

"Boring. Weather's too good."

Albert laughed. "Make the most of it," he said. "It looks as if we're going to get the tail end of that storm from America in the next day or so."

Tea made with condensed milk will always remind me of lighthouses, Jenny thought, savouring every mouthful. A deep happiness settled inside her as they sat round the table, talking about the weather, boats, fishing, gardening, which birds were nesting where, news from the village – all sorts of things. Gareth raided the Trinity House supplies and treated his visitors to exotic food, like tinned pineapple.

Before they left, John took Jenny and Ben up the tower to the lantern room.

"As you can see, I've put the safety blinds down," he said. "When the sun's shining on the lenses, the rays are so powerful they can set your clothes on fire."

Even with the blinds down, the air was stifling. Ben walked round the massive boat-shaped lantern, fascinated by every detail. "This must weigh a ton!" he said.

"Over three-and-a-half tons, if you count the framework. Although it's heavy, the lantern moves ever so easily because it's in that trough of mercury. It makes one complete revolution every sixteen minutes."

Ben and John talked about winding mechanisms, paraffin burners and other technical details while Jenny wandered round the lantern, marvelling at the sheer scale of it all. She was afraid to touch anything in case she left untidy fingerprints. Everything in the lighthouse seemed to have a hard surface which was polished to perfection. "Even on a calm day like today the wind makes a noise up here, doesn't it?" she said as she joined them again. "It must be scary in a storm."

"It certainly tests your nerve on occasion," John replied. "After a while you can tell the force of the wind just by the noise it makes against the glass. If it's humming, it's force five, and then the pitch increases at six, seven and eight." He gave convincing impressions of the noise at those wind speeds and, mercifully, stopped at force eight. Then he showed them how to enter a weather observation in the log book, which the keeper on watch had to do every three hours.

Perhaps I'll be a lighthouse-keeper one day, Jenny thought. I'll be at the South Light, though, because it's closer to the village.

They left just before noon. Outside it had turned into a blisteringly hot day. "How about going to Brazen Ward for a swim?" Jenny suggested.

"I can't. It's my watch soon," said Albert. "Why don't you go along, Ben?"

It was as if Jenny had known Ben all her life. Talking was easy, silences were easy – just being with him was easy.

They navigated their way down the steep zigzag path to Brazen Ward. It appeared to lead nowhere but, like so many paths on Lundy, promised by its existence to lead somewhere.

A watery sing-song floated up from the cove, rising and then falling away again. Dark torpedo-shaped animals lay on the rocks close to the shoreline. Occasionally they splashed into the water and transformed into graceful, grey fish-like creatures.

"I hope you don't mind seals," Jenny said.

Ben looked at them, and smiled. "Of course not, but will the seals mind us?"

The seals didn't seem to mind them at all. Jenny and Ben swam in their T-shirts and shorts. After a while they emerged, dripping and laughing, to sit on warm rocks at the water's edge. All around them seal heads popped out of the water, wide-eyed and inquisitive.

Jenny lay back, totally content. Waves lapped gently just below her feet while gulls wheeled and called overhead, white silhouettes soaring against the shimmering blue sky. She wished every day could be like this.

The tide came in, the seals returned to the sea and Jenny followed Ben up the path. By the time they reached the top, the strong sun had dried their salty clothes to a crisp and they were longing for another swim. They sat down for a rest.

"Fancy *owning* all this!" Ben said.

"I know, wouldn't it be great?" Jenny replied. "Although I think all of us islanders feel we do own it in a way – or perhaps it owns us."

Ben smiled. "Mr Bonham's the real owner, isn't he? What's he like?"

"He's really nice, actually, and very normal," Jenny said. "He inherited Lundy when old Mr Bonham died a few years ago, so he hasn't owned it that long. He has to work on the mainland most of the time, but he comes here as much as he can – sometimes all the way from London just for a weekend! When he's here, he joins in with whatever needs doing, like a proper islander. I'm sure he'd live on Lundy if he could, but I don't think Mrs Bonham likes it quite so much. She misses London a lot, and she has to look after the children when she's here. They're quite a handful, especially Hector. He's the oldest – he must be eight by now – and he's always getting into some sort of trouble. Then there's Camilla, who's about a year younger, and William's just a toddler. Their old nanny refuses to come any more, ever since she had to land at Jenny's Cove in an easterly gale."

"Where's Jenny's Cove?"

"It's on the west side. In fact, it wouldn't take us much longer to go home that way. Come on, I'll show you."

The ponies were grazing near the earthquake zone. Kit still hadn't foaled. Jenny tried to hide her disappointment. The arrival of Kit's foal would have rounded off a perfect day.

They picked their way through the jagged crevasses of the earthquake zone, and sat on a grassy ledge overlooking Jenny's Cove.

"Is Jenny's Cove named after you?" Ben asked.

Jenny laughed. "No, of course not! It was named after a ship which sank here in the eighteenth century, full of treasure. Actually, it's the other way round – I was named after this cove. This used to be Mum and Dad's favourite place."

"How come it isn't any more?"

Jenny didn't even hesitate. "Mum died. She slipped and fell off a cliff when she was helping with a bird survey."

Ben looked her in the eye, direct and sincere. "How awful! How old were you?"

"I was five-and-a-half."

"Do you remember her?"

"Oh yes, especially in my dreams. Sometimes they're so real that I wake up thinking she's still alive. I hate it when that happens. It's awful for Dad too. I think he works all the time to block out the memories. He even sold Mum's pony, a beautiful Lundy mare called Puffin, to someone on the mainland because he couldn't bear to see her every day. Poor Puffin! It wasn't her fault."

Jenny thought fleetingly about Isabella. How different Ben was! He allowed her to be herself. She'd never been able to talk to anyone like she could talk to Ben.

4

As Albert had predicted, the storm from America arrived as a south-westerly gale the following day. The wind howled round the cottage, lifting the curtains even though the windows were fastened. The glass panes creaked and rattled.

Jenny had spent the morning lying on her bed, reading a particularly exciting story. Nothing could break the spell. She'd hardly noticed when Dad had said he was going to the Tavern and asked if she wanted to go too. "No thanks," she'd mumbled, completely engrossed in a different world.

But now she'd finished the book and was suffering the sense of loss she always felt at the end a good story.

Outside, the wind had increased from a howl to a scream. It hammered against the windows, like an outraged giant trying to get in. She felt very alone all of a sudden, and longed for the companionship of the Tavern.

It isn't that far to walk, and I'll be sheltered by walls for most of the way, Jenny thought. She went into the kitchen to find Meg, who sprang up from her bed by the cooker, wagging her tail so enthusiastically that it made her whole body squirm.

"Hello, old girl. Coming to the Tavern with me, eh?" Jenny said, putting on her coat and boots. She opened the door.

Bang! The door flew inwards and sent her flying. Her head hit the hard, cold flagstones.

Wind hurtled into the cottage, breathing life into everything. Coats leapt off their pegs, chairs jumped up and crashed down, the kitchen table turned over, bits of paper flew about like seagulls and crockery fell off the dresser and smashed onto the floor. Meg whined and tried to hide behind the upturned table.

Jenny crawled to the door, desperate to close it as soon as possible. *Heave!* It closed a little. *Heave!* A little bit more. *Heave!* The latch clicked into place, but the wind rattled it angrily. She pushed the large iron bolt home, to make sure. Her head hurt. She sat with her back against the door, trying to recover from the shock.

Meg navigated her way through the wreckage,

wagging her tail uncertainly, and licked Jenny's face.

"Good girl, Meg. It's okay. I'm all right, really I am," Jenny said, hugging Meg's bony, hairy body. She smelled of sheep droppings.

Flash! Kerboom!

Jenny jumped with fright. Meg yelped and dived for cover again. Hailstones showered down, smashing against the cottage with such force that Jenny was sure it would disintegrate. She joined Meg, and held her tight until the thunderstorm passed and the clatter of hail on the roof gave way to the patter of raindrops.

The kitchen was never tidy at the best of times, but now it looked like a disaster zone. Jenny made a valiant attempt to clear it up.

As the wind and rain died down, a new sound drifted into the room – the penetrating, intermittent boom of the South Light foghorn.

Jenny looked out of the window. She saw nothing but grey. I hope the ponies are okay, she thought. How could any animal survive a storm like that? Especially those poor little foals; the wind's strong enough to blow them straight over the cliffs. Oh, I do hope Kit hasn't had her foal! "Come on, Meg. Time to find Dad," she said, pulling on her boots again. She opened the door cautiously, and they stepped out into the gloom.

On impulse Jenny turned right, away from the village and the safety of the Tavern. She had to check the ponies. They were bound to be in the quarries, so it wouldn't take long.

The air was thick with moisture. A warm breeze swirled the mist around, giving crazy impressions of movement and direction. Her bruised head throbbed painfully, and she felt rather sick. She trudged on, guided by some sort of inner auto-pilot.

Jenny searched the quarries and the east side, but found only cattle. Surely the ponies wouldn't be on the west side of the island in this weather? Perhaps they'd pushed a gate open, or jumped out. Perhaps they'd been moved. The sensible thing would be to go back and ask Dad.

Jenny didn't feel sensible, though. She felt panicky. Something was wrong. Maybe her worst fears had been realised, and they'd all been blown over the cliffs into the sea. She'd have to check the west side.

Keeping the Quarter Wall on her left, she walked over the tussocky grass and bracken. It was heavy going.

Meg padded along beside her, giving her the courage to carry on.

Joining the path which ran along the west side, she headed north, still peering intently into the curtains of mist for the outline of a pony.

Nothing. Absolutely nothing.

The ground dipped round some rocks and became lumpy. Jenny knew they'd reached the earthquake zone. Meg crouched down, body quivering.

"What is it, Meg?"

Meg growled, and kept staring straight ahead. Her hackles rose. She growled again, low and menacing.

Midnight galloped out of the mist. He galloped at Meg, head down and ears back.

She yelped and fled.

Nostrils flaring and head held high, Midnight returned, trotting towards Jenny.

Her heart pounded against her ribs. Should she run or stand her ground? A sheer drop of several metres lay behind her. Falling down it would be like falling from the first floor of a house. Jenny stood her ground. "Whoa! Steady!" she said, spreading her arms. Midnight slid to a stop in front of her, snorting and tossing his head. Tentatively, Jenny reached out and touched him. She knew he recognised her, but he still looked agitated.

"There's a good boy. What's the matter?"

Midnight's ears pricked, and his nostrils fluttered.

Looking up, Jenny saw the dark grey outline of a pony coming through the mist, then another and another. They looked enormous, like great ghost horses. The mist had made them seem much larger than life.

More ponies appeared. Jenny counted them, fourteen mares and ten foals in all. She counted again, to see who was missing. Kit.

Midnight whinnied. It was powerful and heartfelt.

A shrill whinny answered him. Kit was nearby, but where?

Slowly and carefully, Jenny started to navigate her way between the jumbled mass of faults and fissures which slumped towards the sea. She could hear waves pounding against the cliffs far below.

Kit stood at the edge of a steep-sided trench, pawing the ground.

Frightened of what she would see, Jenny peered into the trench. A long, white object lay below on some stony turf. It looked like a foal.

Oh no! Jenny's heart was pounding as she slithered, and eventually fell, down the side of the trench, ripping her clothes and skin in the process. She ignored the stinging pain. All she could think about was reaching the foal. There was a chance, after all. The smallest, tiniest chance it was still alive.

The foal tried to stand up, tripped over a rock and fell back awkwardly.

"It's okay, I won't hurt you. I'm your friend," Jenny whispered. Gently, she stroked the wet skin on its little body.

The foal tried to stand up again.

She held it steady while it balanced precariously on spindly legs, twitching and shivering with the effort. It was impossible to imagine something so frail could have survived such a fall, but there didn't seem to be any broken bones – not even a cut.

The foal's legs crumpled, and it sank to the ground again.

I'll have to go and get Dad, Jenny thought. He'll know what to do. The sides of the trench were steep and crumbly, and it was blocked at each end by vertical walls of rock. Jenny walked up and down, looking for the best way out. Slowly, the truth dawned on her: there was no way out! She tried several places, but it was no good. She was well-and-truly stuck.

Jenny said a lot of words which Mrs Hamilton wouldn't have approved of, and went back to the foal. "We'll just have to wait for a search party, little one. I'm sure it won't be long," she said, hoping she was right. Dad was always telling her off for going exploring without telling anyone. If he came home and found her gone, he'd just think she'd gone out for a walk.

The foal, Jenny noticed, was a filly. And, by the look of her navel, she was only a few hours old. She lay on her side, eyes half-closed, exhausted.

"I'll call you Gale, because you were born in one," Jenny said. She took off her coat and put it over the filly. Then she sat on a slab of rock next to her. "My beautiful Gale," she murmured, stroking her thin neck and wispy mane.

The foal fell asleep, but Jenny was cold and wide awake. Gradually, the mist cleared. Midnight and

Kit paced the treacherous ground above, occasionally looking over the side and snorting or whinnying. Although they were no help, Jenny felt comforted by their presence. She talked and sang to the ponies, and tried in vain not to worry.

Small patches of blue appeared between the clouds. A peregrine falcon flew overhead, swift and free, probably going home to its eyrie above the cove. Jenny thought a lot about school, and leaving Midnight and Dad. Gale seemed to be getting weaker. Jenny wanted desperately to help her, but she knew there was nothing she could do but wait.

The clouds above became puffy and edged with orange. Sunset wasn't far off. Jenny gave up talking and singing. Waves of panic swept through her like an incoming tide. She kept checking that Gale was still breathing, terrified that the little foal would die.

Could she hear a dog barking somewhere? Yes, there it was again, she was sure of it. "Meg! Here, Meg!" she shouted. Her voice sounded hollow as it bounced off the walls of the trench. Silence.

Suddenly Meg was above her, looking down. She barked.

"Good girl!" Jenny exclaimed. "Speak up!" Dad always told Meg to speak up if he wanted her to bark when they were moving sheep. "Speak up, Meg!" she repeated.

Meg barked enthusiastically.

"Jenny! Jenny!" Dad's voice. She could hardly believe it.

"Dad! I'm stuck. Over here!" Her voice was weak and shaky.

He came into view, peering over the side with Meg.

Shock waves from pounding hooves juddered through the rocks.

"Watch out, Robert! Here comes that stallion!" Jenny heard Mr Hamilton shout.

Dad and Meg disappeared. Meg yelped, and there was a lot of shouting and swearing.

Jenny couldn't work out what was going on. "Dad!" she screamed. "Where are you?" Nobody seemed to hear. Perhaps Dad and Meg had fallen or been trampled. Perhaps Midnight or Kit had been hurt.

To her relief, Dad's face appeared over the side again. "Are you okay, Jenny?"

"I think so, but I'm *so* cold. How about you? What happened?"

"We're fine. Poor Meg's bolted for home, though. Midnight charged at us, but we've scared him off now. Ben's gone to fetch the others, so we'll have you out in no time." He paused. "Is that a dead foal?"

The panic which Jenny had managed to contain for so long overflowed. "No, b-but she's v-very weak and I-I'm s-so w-worried . . ." She burst into tears.

43

Dad scrambled and slid into the trench, and tried his best to comfort her.

S oon the other islanders arrived with the tractor and trailer, climbing gear and other equipment. They were well practised in rescuing people from the treacherous cliffs around Lundy. Jenny and the foal were soon freed from the trench.

Mrs Hamilton insisted that Jenny needed food, drink and a hot bath as quickly as possible, but Jenny didn't want to leave Gale. "She needs food and warmth even more than I do," she protested.

Dad and Ben promised they'd look after her.

Unable to argue any more, she was lifted onto the trailer. Mrs Hamilton got on beside her and held her close. Jenny could hardly bear to look at Gale lying on the grass. "Take care of her!" she shouted to Dad as Mr Hamilton started the tractor.

"Don't worry, I've nursed lots of lambs in my time," Dad called back.

His remark wasn't as comforting as it was meant to be. Jenny had often helped her dad, and she'd seen enough lambs to know that if they didn't drink their mother's milk soon after birth they often didn't make it.

5

When Jenny woke up it was pitch black and completely quiet. Shouldn't she be worried about something? She rolled over. *Ouch!* Why did she ache all over?

"Gale!" she said.

She felt for the torch on the floor beside her bed, turned it on and squinted at her watch. Half-past-three in the morning.

Trying to ignore her protesting muscles, she carefully got out of bed and hobbled around, collecting and putting on clothes as quickly as possible. This must be what it's like to be old, she thought. Suddenly everything's difficult – even simple things, like putting on socks.

By fading torchlight, Jenny crept through the kitchen, out of the cottage and over to the farmyard. The air felt cool and crisp. Stars peppered the sky.

Thin slivers of light shone from the split between the stable doors leading to the old cattle shed – "the shippen" everyone called it. This was where Dad had said they'd taken Gale last night. He'd told Jenny that Gale was doing well and there was nothing to worry about, but he may have said that so she'd sleep. She wanted to see for herself.

To her surprise, the doors were locked. She peered through a crack between the upper and lower halves. It was hard to see in the semi-darkness, but the shape she could make out didn't look like a foal. The animal made a funny sort of bleating noise, just like a goat. "Ermintrude?" Jenny said in disbelief.

Ben's voice answered from inside the shed. "Jenny? What are you doing? You're supposed to be asleep!"

"I know, but I woke up again. How's Gale?"

"Who?"

"The foal. I've called her Gale, because she was born in one."

"Oh, I see. Good name," Ben said. "She's fine. Hang on a minute. You can come and see for yourself." There was a rustling sound, and then a grating noise as the bolts on the door were undone. "Sorry, the bottom one will only stay closed if the top one's locked," he explained.

Gale lay on a thick bed of straw in the corner of the shed. Her body was covered with blankets, leaving only her head visible. A lamp hanging from a beam nearby gave off a warm glow.

Jenny knelt beside the foal and stroked her neck. It felt warm and silky.

Ben knelt beside her. "See? There's no need to worry. You can go back to bed now."

"Maah!" Ermintrude called to a tiny fawn-coloured creature lying in the straw.

"Oh, I've just realised! Clever old Ermintrude's had a kid. When did that happen?" Jenny asked.

"Yesterday. Perfect timing, because she had lots of that rich first milk, so I've been giving some to Gale. Not quite as good as her own mother's milk, of course, but according to Mrs Hamilton it's the next best thing. She said a famous racehorse was reared on goat's milk after its mother died."

Jenny's heart lurched. "Kit isn't dead, is she?"

"No, she's in the shed next door. Can't you hear her pacing around?

Jenny had heard something, but she hadn't realised it was Kit. Dad often kept cattle in that shed. "Why isn't she in here? She should be with her foal."

"I know, but Gale was far too weak to get up and

suck, and Kit was so agitated we thought she'd trample her to death."

"Oh," Jenny said. Each time one question was answered, lots more popped into her head. "How did you manage to feed Gale?"

"Mrs Hamilton helped me. She showed me how to milk a goat, for a start. I've never milked one before, but luckily Ermintrude was very good. Then, of course, we had the problem of getting the milk from the bucket and into Gale, but Mrs Hamilton had a brainwave. She got one of her rubber cleaning gloves, tied the fingers up and put a hole in the end of the thumb with a hat pin. Look, a home-made teat! Isn't that clever? Gale took to it straight away. I didn't realise a little thing like her could drink so much."

Jenny couldn't help feeling a bit jealous. She wished she'd been the one to give Gale her first feed.

There was a piercing whinny from the shed next door. Gale heard it, opened her eyes and tried to struggle to her feet. Jenny and Ben removed her blankets and helped her. She stood there for a few seconds before her legs crumpled and she sank into the straw. They helped her up again, and this time she stood for longer before her legs gave way. Each time they lifted her she became stronger and more coordinated. Before long, she was taking hesitant, dainty steps. She tottered up to Jenny and nuzzled her hopefully.

Jenny didn't think she'd ever felt such love for anything. "She's looking for some milk," she whispered.

Ben grinned. "Time to milk Ermintrude."

Kit whinnied again, and this time Gale attempted a short, high-pitched reply. Kit responded by whinnying frantically. They could hear her charging around the shed. She whinnied again. An answer came immediately from somewhere beyond the farm buildings, like a low echo. By the sounds of it, Midnight had jumped the Quarter Wall and was trying to find her.

"Oh dear, we don't need Midnight putting a spanner in the works," Jenny said. "Do you think we dare put Kit in here with Gale? It doesn't seem right to keep them apart now that Gale's so much stronger, and she'll be much better off with her mother's milk."

"Well, we'll have to sooner or later, I suppose," said Ben. "How shall we move her, though? It took about nine of us to round her up and chase her down here."

"I expect that was the problem," Jenny replied. "Too many people making too much noise. If a horse panics it can't think properly, then it's much more difficult to handle."

"How come you know so much about horses?" Ben asked.

"The ponies have taught me. I spend all my spare

time with them, you see." Jenny walked towards the door. Gale tried to follow her. "Oh no you don't, little one," Jenny said, steering her back into the far corner. Exhausted by all the exercise, Gale lay down on top of the blankets.

"Okay," Ben said decisively. "Let's put Ermintrude and her kid somewhere safe, then we can let Kit in here."

Jenny wondered whether he felt as confident as he sounded, but it was nice not to have made the final decision. If things went wrong, at least she wouldn't feel it was entirely her fault.

With some food as a bribe, they coaxed Ermintrude and her baby into a small shed. Jenny noticed that the sky had become lighter. It would soon be daytime.

Cautiously, they opened the top half of Kit's stable door. She walked towards them. Her body was shivering and feathered with sweat.

"Right, I'll open this door and you open the door to the shippen," Ben said. "Then stand back and pray everything goes according to plan."

Jenny only just had time to open the shippen door before Kit rushed out of her shed. She charged round the yard in the cold half-light, skidding at the corners, whinnying frantically. Midnight's ardent replies were much closer this time.

We shouldn't have done this, Jenny thought helplessly. Kit's much too het up to be with Gale. She's bound to knock her over or trample her. Perhaps she won't even recognise her own foal; we may have left it too late. Jenny was just about to run and shut the door again when a tiny, shrill whinny came from the shippen.

Kit slithered to a halt. She stared intently at the open double door, and her nostrils flickered. Then she walked forwards hesitantly, drawn by the possibility that the thing she wanted most in the world was inside, but fearful of the unknown.

The foal whinnied again. Kit's answer was rumbling and tender as she went into the shed. It was too late to do anything now, except hope for the best.

Jenny and Ben listened anxiously for squeals and bangs, but only gentle rustles and horsey murmurings came out of the shed, so they tiptoed closer to have a look.

Gale was nursing with eager sucking noises, her fluffy silver tail swishing enthusiastically. Kit nuzzled the foal's bottom as it drank, whickering affectionately.

Happiness, love and grief swept through Jenny as she stood watching the idyllic scene. Gale had a mother to love her and look after her now.

*

The peace was shattered by the arrival of Midnight. He stood at the gate into the yard, whinnying loudly and pawing at the bars in a frenzy of frustration. Kit called to him eagerly in reply. Before Ben and Jenny could decide what to do, Midnight jumped the gate from a standstill.

"Quick! Get out of here!" Ben exclaimed, diving into Kit's old stable. "Come on, Jenny! Hurry!"

Jenny didn't move. "Did you see that? Isn't he the most amazing jumper?" she said, as Midnight clattered towards her.

"Come *on!*" Ben urged. "He's a killer, that horse! Everyone says so."

She stood still and held out her hand. "Well, I certainly don't. He's lovely. Aren't you, boy?"

Midnight arched his neck and snorted, eyes blazing in the pink light of dawn. Then he walked towards her, and brushed her hand with his muzzle before greeting Kit over the shippen door with happy grunts and squeals. Jenny stroked his neck. He quivered, relaxing at her touch.

"Blimey!" said Ben, venturing out of his hiding place. "I'd never have believed it!"

Midnight shied away, then faced him and pinned back his ears.

Ben jumped backwards. "See what I mean? They were right."

"Nonsense," Jenny said, although she had to admit Midnight did look pretty scary when he wanted to. "Who are 'they', anyway? Who's been saying he's a killer?"

Ben looked embarrassed. "Well, quite a few people, really. They were all talking last night, after they'd rescued you. He kept trying to attack us when we were lifting Gale onto the trailer."

"I expect he was just trying to protect his foal. After all, he didn't know why you were taking her away. He probably thought you were kidnapping her rather than trying to save her life."

Ben didn't look convinced. "Okay, then, what about the first time we met?"

Jenny was puzzled.

"Midnight was chasing you, don't you remember? Dad was telling everyone about it."

"No! He's got it all wrong!" Jenny exclaimed. "You see, Midnight wasn't chasing me, he was *following* me! You actually saw the most wonderful thing: the moment he followed me for the first time. It's taken years for him to trust me that much. I spent hours watching the herd before he came up and let me touch him, and now he even lets me – oh, it's no use. You wouldn't believe it, anyway."

"Try me."

"He lets me ride him."

"What, properly? With a saddle and bridle?"

Jenny sighed wistfully. "No, I haven't even got a head collar. I just hop on his back and ride him around when he's grazing with the herd sometimes. I can't steer him or anything." An awful thought struck her. "You won't tell anyone, will you? I'm afraid they'll stop me."

"From the way they were talking last night, that'll be the least of your worries. If they can catch him, they're planning on shipping him to the mainland. They've been trying to for some time, apparently, because all the ponies are becoming too closely related. They want to get a new stallion in."

Jenny was horrified. "We'd better get him out of here fast, before anyone wakes up! You open the gate, and I'll drive him out."

Ben got to the gate, turned back and hissed frantically, "Your dad's coming! I'll try to stall him while you hide Midnight!"

Easier said than done! Jenny thought. She looked around the yard in a panic, but saw no easy hiding place for a wild stallion she couldn't lead. Her only hope was the shippen, with Kit and Gale. It was a risk, but there was no option. She opened the door.

Kit made to rush out, but then remembered her foal was inside, so rushed back in, hotly followed by Midnight.

Jenny slammed the doors shut behind the ponies, and forced the rusty bolts home just as Dad walked in through the gate, followed by Ben making "I'm sorry" signs.

There was a terrible commotion inside the shed: banging, sliding, squealing scraping and a thudding noise, like falling rocks. Then a few scuffles, a whinny, silence.

"Is everything all right in there?" Dad asked, rushing over.

Jenny fumbled with the stubborn bolts. She was pretty certain everything wasn't all right. Gale had probably been trampled to death, for a start. She flung the top door open and said, "You look, Dad. I can't bear to. I'm sorry, it was a stupid idea."

Dad looked in. "All well, as far as I can see. Well done for reuniting them. It wasn't a stupid idea at all. She's a bonny little thing, isn't she?"

"What? But . . ."

"Are you okay, Jenny?" Dad asked. "You seem a bit delirious. Perhaps you should go back to bed."

Ben, Dad and Jenny stood there, peering into the dusty shippen.

Perhaps I *have* gone potty, Jenny thought. She could see Kit and Gale standing at the far end, apparently unharmed. Midnight had vanished. At the back there was an old wall which was over two metres high.

Beyond, there was a field called Pig's Paradise. Kit looked towards Pig's Paradise, and whinnied.

Jenny and Ben smiled at each other.

He can't have – he must have! Midnight had jumped the wall.

6

Mrs Hamilton liked nothing better than a party. Birthdays were her speciality, and her cakes were legendary.

Jenny's birthday party was a Friday lunchtime barbecue on the Landing Beach. Everyone on the island was invited, residents and visitors alike. Fortunately it wasn't a boat day.

By midday it seemed as if the entire population of the island was on the beach, drinking, talking, swimming and cooking sausages over a driftwood fire. The sun shone down on them from a cloudless sky.

This is the best birthday ever, Jenny thought as she joined the party. She was especially pleased to see that

Dad had managed to take a break from turning hay. He'd given her a riding hat, some creamy-coloured jodhpurs and a big birthday hug at breakfast time. Then, full of apologies, he'd rushed off to the hay field. Jenny knew he'd had no option; every hour counted when making hay, especially when it was nearly ready to harvest.

Still, she'd had the most wonderful morning. Mr and Mrs Hamilton had given her a pair of smart brown leather riding boots, and Albert had invited her to morning tea at the South Light, where he'd given her a book . . . *Then*, as she'd been walking down the Beach Road a moment ago, the most amazing thing had happened! She still couldn't really believe it. Mr Bonham had stopped her outside Millcombe, wished her a happy birthday and had *given* her Gale as a birthday present – just like that! *Gale was her pony!* She'd be able to watch her grow up, look after her, groom her, train her and, eventually, ride her – like Mum had with Puffin. Mr Bonham had told her that Puffin was Kit's older sister, and therefore Gale's aunt. He'd said it would be lovely to see Jenny carry on the "Medway tradition" of owning a pony on Lundy. Jenny had decided there and then that Mr Bonham was one of the nicest people in the world – along with Albert and Dad, of course.

Dad was the first person Jenny told about Gale. He

grinned, hugged her and said he was thrilled, but he didn't look as surprised as he should have, somehow. Perhaps Mr Bonham had consulted him beforehand. The news about Gale spread quickly, and soon everyone was talking about Jenny's fantastic birthday present. She was given more gifts as the party went on: a drawing, sweets, some Lundy stamps, a carved piece of driftwood and, best of all, a beautiful hand-knitted yellow polo neck sweater from Sheila. Although it was a baking hot day, Jenny couldn't resist trying it on for size. It fitted perfectly, with just enough room for growth. She noticed Sheila and Dad exchanging special smiles, and wondered whether this was another present he'd known about.

Most people gave her some sort of gift. Ben didn't, though. She told herself she shouldn't care. Presents weren't important, and she'd had more than her fair share. But a present from Ben, even something small like an interesting shell from the beach, would have meant so much. Never mind. It was wrong of her to expect anything.

After lunch, most of the men, including Ben, left to lend a hand carting the hay into the barn. Jenny helped Mr and Mrs Hamilton clear up the party debris. The tractor and trailer were being used for haymaking, so everything had to be carried up the Beach Road by hand. When they reached the Hotel, Mrs Hamilton excused Jenny from any further work because it was her birthday.

I wish every day could be like this, she thought as she went to find the ponies. Her birthday wouldn't be complete without seeing them.

On the way she met the tractor with a load of hay destined for the barn. Ben was perched on top of the load, grinning broadly and obviously loving every minute of the hot, dusty, exhausting work. Mr Bonham was up there with him, and they both waved.

"Hello, birthday girl!" Ben called down to her. "Want a ride?"

"No thanks! I'm off to see Gale!" she replied.

They grinned and gave a thumbs up sign as the trailer carried them away down the track towards the village.

The ponies were lazing around on top of the hill at the centre of the island, making the most of a breeze from any direction in the scorching heat. Some were standing, dozing on their feet, and others were lying down. A few, including Midnight, were lying flat out.

Midnight, sensing Jenny's presence, lifted his head lazily and then, reluctantly, scrambled to his feet. As she went up to him he swished his tail and walked away with his ears back, making it perfectly clear that he objected to being woken from his siesta.

Gale, on the other hand, seemed delighted to see

Jenny. She trotted up for a cuddle, uttering short high-pitched whinnies. She was now a spirited, inquisitive foal, with a solid little body and Midnight's deep blue eyes.

"Hello, Gale," Jenny said, stroking her warm, velvety neck. "Guess what? I'm your new owner." Saying it didn't make it any more believable. How could she ever claim to own something so beautiful?

Gale stood contentedly, enjoying the attention, with no concept of what ownership meant or why it should matter to her.

After a while Midnight wandered up. He nudged Jenny.

"Why, I do believe you're jealous!" she said, stroking him with her other arm. "It doesn't mean I love you any less because I own Gale, you know. It's lucky I've got two arms, isn't it? If I stroke both of you at the same time, neither of you will feel left out."

By the time Jenny left the ponies she could no longer hear the distant drone of the tractor, and the hay field was empty – stripped bare, like a shorn sheep. The sweet smell of fresh hay hung in the air as she made her way home.

In the kitchen there was a note from her dad, saying he'd gone to the Tavern. After washing quickly, and putting on her best jeans and shirt, she went to join him.

A party was already in full swing. To Jenny's slight embarrassment, she was immediately the centre of attention. Mrs Hamilton played *Happy Birthday* on the piano, and everyone sang along, followed by three cheers led by Mr Hamilton. Then he sang his party piece, which the islanders called *The Hartland Song,* and they joined in the chorus with great gusto.

Several others took a turn with songs, stories or poems, including Albert, who gave a hilarious recital of *The Lion and Albert* and *The Return of Albert.*

The singing became louder as the evening wore on. Ben stood next to Jenny, his arm linked with hers. She felt light-headed and happy.

Sheila put plates of sandwiches and hot sausage rolls on the counter. Conversation subsided to a murmur as everybody began eating. Jenny and Ben found a couple of seats in the corner.

"Oh, that's better!" Ben sat down. He looked weary, and his face glowed with sunburn. There were angry red blisters on his hands.

"Still want to be a farmer?" Jenny teased.

"You bet! Today's been brilliant!"

Jenny's dad stood up and banged on a table. Everyone was surprised into silence. "I'd like to propose a toast to my beautiful daughter, Jenny." He looked straight at her, making her blush. "You'll always be my sunshine," he said, his usual reserve softened by drink. "All the very best!"

"To Jenny!" everyone chorused. *"All the very best!"* They drank her health enthusiastically.

"And I'd like to propose a toast to the haymakers. Thanks for all your help. It would have been a long, lonely job without you," he added.

"To the haymakers!"

Dad appeared to be enjoying himself. "And to Sheila and Mrs Hamilton for feeding us all."

A communal cry of *"To the cooks!"* nearly raised the roof.

Mrs Hamilton carried in a birthday cake with candles flickering on top. It was a work of art. She'd made it in the shape of a pony, with a golden marzipan body and chocolate mane and tail. Perhaps Mrs Hamilton had known about Jenny's surprise birthday present too. It was so beautiful that Jenny didn't want to cut it, but everybody was watching expectantly. She removed the candles, leaving deep, ugly craters in the marzipan. Then she closed her eyes and plunged the knife into the cake, making a fervent wish as she did so.

Happy Birthday was sung for the third time that day, louder than ever.

"Give us a tune, Jenny!" Batty roared from the other side of the room. "How about some jolly old Scott Joplin? You're awfully good at that!"

Friendly hands pushed Jenny towards the piano, crowding in and then thinning out like a retreating wave, leaving a respectful space around the piano. Jenny sat down on the stool and spent a long time adjusting it to the right height while the nervousness she always felt before playing to an audience subsided. Without saying anything, she launched straight into her favourite ragtime tune, *The Maple Leaf Rag,* and her nerves evaporated.

The piano was so familiar that Jenny could have hit the right notes with her eyes closed. She'd been playing it since she was six, under the careful tuition of Mrs Hamilton, and she was allowed to practise whenever the Tavern was closed. When she knew Mrs Hamilton was listening, she played Mozart, Beethoven and other classical composers. When she thought she could get away with it, she switched to Scott Joplin or tried to work out the tunes of pop songs she'd heard on the radio.

As she played the final chord, everybody clapped, and over the general noise Batty bellowed, "Bravo! Encore!"

"This one's for Dad. It's called *You Are My Sunshine,*" Jenny said.

When the chorus came around, Dad joined her and, to everybody's surprise, led the singing.

Jenny couldn't help remembering Mum sitting at the same piano, playing the same tune, while she and Dad sang together – his strong, warm hand holding hers, giving her confidence. She'd forgotten how wonderful Dad's voice was. Since the accident he'd hardly sung at all. The keyboards became a blur as happy memories she'd tried so hard to forget were coaxed out of their hiding place by the music.

After they'd finished there was silence for a few seconds before the Tavern erupted with applause. Dad's hand reached out for Jenny's, and pulled her to her feet so they could take a bow. Then he kissed her hand and gave her a hug. He smelled of beer and cigarettes. "I love you," she whispered, pressing her face against his broad chest.

"Where did you learn to sing like that? You were amazing!" Sheila's voice broke through the din in the background.

Dad released Jenny. His whole face lit up in a smile as he met Sheila's eyes and gave her a hug.

Jenny looked away, her special moment cut short. The Tavern was now completely packed. It was difficult to move, and it looked as if several people were intent on making the party last until dawn. She tapped Dad on the shoulder. "Dad?"

He pulled away from Sheila, looking embarrassed. "Sorry, love. Er, I was just . . ."

Jenny tried to look as if she didn't mind at all. "Don't worry. I'm off home now. Thanks for a lovely birthday."

"Goodnight, love. Are you sure you'll be all right by yourself? Would you like me to come with you?" Dad replied.

Jenny hated the thought of being alone in the cottage, but she could see he didn't want to leave. "No, I'll be fine. Night, night."

"Night, love. Sleep well."

Cool, hay-laden air greeted Jenny as she left the Tavern. The night was calm and clear, but still warm enough for Jenny to feel comfortable wearing a thin shirt. She stood for a moment, looking up at the stars.

The Tavern door banged shut, making her jump. She swung round.

Ben hurried towards her. "Thank goodness you're still here! I thought you'd gone home," he said. "I've got a birthday present for you."

He'd remembered!

He took her hand. "Come on, it's in the Church. I didn't know where else to hide it."

Jenny waited by the heavy oak door of the Church while Ben went in to get her mysterious gift. He returned, holding a parcel.

"Let's go outside," he whispered.

"Okay," Jenny whispered back, wondering why it didn't seem right to talk normally in church.

They walked a short distance, and then Ben sat down on the grass. Jenny sat beside him on the spongy turf. The moon bathed everything in silvery light, washing out all the normal colours.

"Happy birthday," Ben said, and he handed her a crinkled brown paper parcel tied up with string.

It was quite flat, but knobbly, and heavier than she'd expected. She had no idea what it could be. Trying to hide her eagerness, she eased off the string.

A tangled mass of knotted rope slid from the package. Jenny felt confused. Had Ben played some sort of joke on her?

"I hope you like it. I made it myself, but I think it'll work okay. I got the rope from a fisherman, in return for helping him for an afternoon."

What on earth can I say? Jenny thought. I can't say I love it when I don't even know what it is. She lifted the rope by the largest knot, and suddenly everything fell into shape. "Oh!" she exclaimed. "A rope halter for Midnight. It's just what I need! Thank you *so much*!"

"Glad you like it," Ben said, grinning.

They sat there in companionable silence. Music drifted up from the Tavern. In the distance, intermittent flashes came from lighthouses dotted along the North Devon coast.

Jenny couldn't think of anywhere else she'd rather be. Ben seemed to have a habit of making days perfect.

7

The sun shone from a deep blue sky, making the sea sparkle. Jenny looked longingly out of the large sash window of the Hotel bedroom she was supposed to be cleaning.

It's so unfair, she thought. I live here all year round, but just when the weather's good, the days are long and lots of people are enjoying themselves, I have to work in the boring old Hotel. I wish I could work outside with Ben.

She couldn't stop thinking about Ben and the halter he'd given her. It was her most prized possession – even more special than her riding clothes. Actually, Gale had been her best present, of course. But she couldn't get her head round a pony being a thing you could possess – not in the same way as clothes or a halter made by a good friend, anyway. The halter was precious because Ben had made it especially for her. It was also precious because it held the key to Midnight's future. If everything went according to plan, she'd now be able to tame him and show everyone what a wonderful pony he was. Then he'd be allowed to stay on Lundy forever, and she'd be able to ride him all over the island. They'd be inseparable. And if he couldn't be the herd stallion any more, she'd keep him in St Helen's Field, by the cottage. Perhaps he'd be able to have Rosie for company . . .

"Jenny! Haven't you finished that room yet? Do hurry up! Sheila needs help in the kitchen." Mrs Hamilton's head appeared round the bedroom door. "My goodness! You haven't even made the bed yet. Get a move on, girl!"

Rudely awakened from her glorious daydream, Jenny leapt to the bed and hurriedly rearranged the sheets and blankets, taking care to smooth down the bits that showed. Then she rushed downstairs to the kitchen.

By the evening, Jenny felt so weary her bones ached. All she really wanted to do was lie on her bed and read, but she'd promised herself she'd start training Midnight with the halter. She had no idea how long it took to break a wild pony, but she knew she should make a start as soon as possible. She'd been trying hard not to think about school in September because it made her feel ill with worry. Now, however, she had to face up to the fact that time was running out. Midnight had to be fully trained by the end of the summer holidays.

Reluctantly she got off her bed, opened the top drawer of her chest of drawers and took the halter from its hiding place under her pants, vests and socks. It was made from one long piece of rope, spliced and knotted into shape. Jenny wound the whole thing round her waist and put her coat on, zipping it up with difficulty.

Her dad was reading a farming magazine at the kitchen table, surrounded by the dirty dishes from tea. The radio crackled and whined in its efforts to pick up a signal from the mainland.

Jenny edged out of her bedroom door, and crept round the side of the kitchen.

"Going out again?" Dad asked. "Don't be late. I thought you were looking rather tired at teatime." His eyes didn't leave the page he was reading.

"I'm fine. Won't be long," Jenny said. Then she was out of the door, and away.

For the first time in her life, Jenny was nervous as she approached Midnight. Sensing it instantly, he snorted at the halter in her hand, and backed away.

Just act normally, you fool, Jenny told herself. She stood looking out to sea, ignoring Midnight and the ponies, trying to calm herself. Before long she felt warm breath on her hand. It wasn't Midnight, it was Gale.

As Jenny cuddled Gale, she realised the foal was taking no notice of the halter swinging from her arm. Carefully, she slipped the rope round Gale's neck. Easy! The headpiece was far too big for the little foal, but she didn't seem to mind the rope round her neck at all. She followed Jenny around like a faithful puppy.

True to form, Midnight's curiosity got the better of him. He edged closer, seeking attention.

"You want to have a go too, do you?" Jenny asked. She rubbed Midnight's neck with her hand until he relaxed. Then she rubbed his neck with the rope, and managed to drop the end of the rope over his neck to form a loop. Every movement was slow and deliberate.

Now for the tricky part, Jenny thought, trying to sort out the headpiece with one hand while holding onto the neck rope with the other. Midnight turned his head to have a look at what she was doing, and pushed his nose straight into the nosepiece of the halter. Jenny couldn't believe her luck. Before he could have second thoughts, she quickly eased the remains of the halter over his ears. It was on!

Instantly aware of the strange thing around his head, Midnight snorted in alarm and shied away. Jenny grabbed hold of the rope around his neck, and the loose end whipped round, hitting his flank. He pulled back in earnest, bracing himself against the rope. Jenny hung on doggedly, but she was no match for the stallion. He reared up, fighting against the pressure around his head, and the rope jerked savagely from Jenny's hand. She caught a glimpse of his hooves and his wild eye, and then he galloped off with the long rope trailing between his legs.

"*Ouch!*" wailed Jenny, nursing her hand. "Ouch! Ouch! Ouch!" The mares and foals, alarmed by Midnight's sudden departure, galloped after the stallion in an excited flurry.

Jenny realised she now had a serious problem; her halter was still on Midnight, and she couldn't leave it there. She trudged after the ponies for what seemed like ages. As she'd feared, Midnight kept a safe distance from her. Several times he trod on the rope, but the halter stayed firmly on his head.

Jenny was so tired she couldn't think straight. The ponies had reached the main track, and the sun was setting. She decided to admit defeat. As she turned for home, Midnight walked towards her, stopped at a marker stone and rubbed his head against it, working the halter loose over his ears. It flopped to the ground. He picked it up in his teeth, shook it fiercely and dropped it on the track a couple of yards from her, giving her a withering look as if to say, "That's what I think of your stupid idea!" Then he walked away to join his mares.

The halter lay crumpled in the dust, inert and harmless. Jenny picked it up, and made her way home – mind numb, legs like jelly and dreams shattered.

*

"Sugar lumps, that's what you need," said Ben after Jenny had told him about her disastrous training session. "Grandpa used to say that horses will do anything for sugar. He worked with farm horses, you see. I remember him smothering a metal bit in treacle to get a young horse to accept it. After a while that horse shoved its head into the bridle, no problem. If you want Midnight to like the halter, you should give him something nice while he's wearing it."

"You're a genius!" Jenny exclaimed. "We've got boxes of sugar lumps in the Hotel kitchen. The ones that are left in the bowls after the guests have finished are usually put in the pig swill, so I'm sure it wouldn't matter if I took them instead." She hadn't imagined the solution to her problem would be so simple.

The following day was a boat day. As usual, Jenny helped in the Hotel kitchen at lunch time and in the Tea Garden in the afternoon. This gave her plenty of opportunity to divert leftover sugar lumps into the pockets of her shorts while she was clearing the tables.

By the time she got home, some of the sugar lumps had worn away to a sticky dust. She carefully salvaged what she could and transferred them into a paper bag. Then she changed, washed her shorts, hung them to dry, picked up the halter and went to find Midnight.

The ponies were loafing around on the west side, making the most of the evening sunshine and a slight south-westerly breeze which kept the flies at bay. They looked sleek, fat and content.

Trying to stay calm, Jenny hid the halter behind a rock and walked slowly towards the herd. As usual, it wasn't Midnight who came up first, but Gale. Jenny stroked her and offered her a sugar lump. The little foal sniffed it, explored it delicately with her lips and then nibbled it tentatively. Soon she was munching happily, and looking around for more.

Jenny laughed with delight. "You like sweeties, do you?" she asked, fondling Gale's soft, stumpy mane.

Midnight couldn't resist investigating what his daughter was eating with such obvious enjoyment. He snuffled at the bag, and drew back suspiciously when it rustled.

Jenny put a sugar lump on the palm of her hand and held it flat, remembering a photo in one of her pony books with the caption, "The correct way to offer a titbit".

Like Gale, Midnight investigated the sugar lump with his lips, and then took it between his teeth. *Crunch!* Eagerly he searched for more in the bag, and pinned his ears back at Gale when she tried to do likewise.

"Not so fast, Sunshine!" Jenny said. "You've got to earn your treats." She went to pick up the halter, and Midnight followed close behind. Carefully, she put a sugar lump on her palm, and placed the nose loop of the halter above it so he'd have to push his nose through it to get his reward. It worked perfectly, and he had another lump as she slipped the halter over his ears. He snorted when he felt the rope tighten over his head, and started to pull back, but Jenny was ready with more sugar.

Jenny put the bag in her left hand, held the rope in her right hand and walked forwards. For an awful moment, Midnight hesitated. The rope went tight, and he pulled backwards. Quickly, she offered a sugar lump a few inches in front of his nose, and he walked towards her instead.

After a few minutes of leading round in circles, there were only two sugar lumps left. Jenny gave them as a final reward once she'd eased the halter off.

Crunch! Crunch! Crunch! Sticky saliva dribbled from Midnight's mouth. He raised his head and curled his top lip, savouring the intense taste of pure sugar.

Jenny ran across Ackland's Moor, laughing and leaping. Ben's idea had worked brilliantly! She couldn't wait to tell him. Midnight liked her again! Why hadn't she thought of sugar lumps before? They made horse training so easy!

Midnight's training sessions went pretty well for a few days. Soon he was greeting Jenny with a whinny and running to her eagerly – a bit too eagerly sometimes, she felt. He'd started approaching visitors in a similar fashion as well, presumably to see whether they also carried sugar lumps. Some had even reported he'd "attacked" them.

Jenny was sure he hadn't actually attacked anyone, but it wasn't doing his reputation any good. She'd have to start riding him as soon as possible, to prove how wonderful he really was.

As she lay awake one night, she imagined riding Midnight down the High Street to the Tavern. A crowd of islanders would be gathered outside, speechless with admiration, or perhaps clapping – she hadn't quite decided which she preferred. Mr Bonham would be standing at the door to the Tavern, smiling. Midnight would halt in front of him, like a show pony in front of the judge.

"I can see that pony means the world to you, Jenny," he would say. "He can't possibly be shipped to the mainland now that he's been tamed. I'd like to give him to you, as a thank you for all your hard work. You can ride him until Gale's old enough to be broken in, and then he can have a happy retirement here on the island. Just one thing, though, I'm afraid you won't be able to go to school. You'll have to stay here and look after your ponies."

"Oh, thank you, Mr Bonham," she'd say, and she'd

dismount and shake his hand – or perhaps he'd kiss her lightly on the cheek, like grown-ups did.

That was her fantasy. The reality was that the riding part of Midnight's training wasn't going at all well. She just couldn't seem to get him to understand what she wanted, no matter how much she squeezed with her legs or pulled on the halter rope. It ended up with him getting annoyed and her getting frustrated to the point of despair. What she needed was someone to lead Midnight while she rode him. She decided to ask Ben to help. Then she lay awake for a long time, worrying about school, Midnight and the amount of time Sheila had been spending with Dad recently.

The following evening Jenny and Ben went to find Midnight. The weather was damp and overcast. Midnight and some of the mares and foals were at the northern entrance to the quarries, near Halfway Wall. Nobody was about. Ideal.

"Shall I give you a leg-up?" Ben asked.

"I don't know. I usually just get on from a rock or broken-down wall."

"It's really easy. Just stand facing him and lift your left leg so I can hold your ankle – yes, like that. Then we go one, two, three, hup!"

Jenny felt herself rise into the air with tremendous

force. She nearly sailed right over Midnight's back, but grabbed hold of a handful of mane and somehow managed to land on top of him. She could tell he wasn't at all happy. "I think I'd better get down," she said nervously.

Ben smiled up at her, holding the halter rope loosely across the palm of his hand. "Nonsense! You'll be fine! I've got hold of him, look."

Everything happened very fast after that. There was a whinny from Middle Park, on the other side of Halfway Wall. Midnight's head shot up, and he whinnied back. Jenny felt him quivering. He broke away from Ben's loose hold, and started trotting purposefully towards the wall. It was jerky and uncomfortable, and Jenny clung onto his mane with all her strength as she wobbled around on his slippery back.

"Hey! Come back! Whoa! Slow down!" Ben yelled, running behind them.

"Shut up, Ben! You're not helping!" Jenny shouted.

"What? I can't hear you!" Ben's voice was further away now. "Oh, cripes! Hang on, Jenny!"

Midnight's pace quickened and became smoother. Jenny could see his shoulders working like pistons below her. She felt his muscles bunch and stretch, creating raw, uncontrollable power.

A solid grey line loomed ahead, blurred through Jenny's watering eyes. A wall, she thought hopelessly.

Halfway Wall! He must stop! *He must!*

The grey line became large, dark and unavoidable. She could just make out the outline of the slate stile by the Logan Stone. At least if they jumped the stile it wouldn't be quite so high, but if Midnight swerved to the right at the last minute they could both end up over the cliffs.

Midnight's ears pricked forward and he accelerated, full of confidence. I'm going to die, Jenny thought. She felt remarkably calm about it – resigned to her fate.

His neck stretched out, and she felt a tremendous surge beneath her. They flew through the air, held together by two handfuls of mane. The blotchy granite wall flashed beneath them, and then they started falling back down again. Jenny closed her eyes, and waited for the end.

Midnight landed with a jolt, jerking Jenny forward over his neck, then back again, so she sprawled over his back as he galloped on without a pause. Her muscles screamed with the effort of hanging on and she could taste blood in her mouth, but she was still on board.

A bunch of mares and foals came galloping up to meet them. Midnight slowed to a high-stepping, jarring trot, which was much more scary and uncomfortable than his gallop.

All Jenny's strength had gone. She felt like a rag doll. She'd have to let go. Hitting the ground would hurt, but at least that would be the end of it.

Midnight's head dropped abruptly. He stopped. Jenny lay halfway up his neck, knowing she'd gone beyond the point of no return. She slid off in slow motion and lay, rather dazed, in a large clump of heather.

He stood with his neck arched downwards, trying in vain to pull his head up. He'd trodden on the trailing rope of the halter with a hind hoof. It was pinning his head to the ground.

As quickly as she could, Jenny worked at the halter until it was loose enough to slip over Midnight's ears, then she took it off.

He shook his head, and stood still for a moment, looking at her. Then he trotted away jauntily to his breakaway herd.

Jenny sat on the prickly heather, relishing the fact it didn't move. She'd never felt such a mixture of emotions: terror, relief, pain, joy, exasperation and exhilaration all rolled into one. I've galloped on Midnight! I've jumped on Midnight! Oh, it was amazing! Never again, though, she thought. Never, ever, again!

"Jenny! Jenny! Are you all right? I'm so sorry!" Ben ran up, gasping and red in the face.

"Battered, bruised, but no broken bones." Jenny's voice echoed in her throbbing head. "It wasn't your fault. He'd have run off anyway, to get to the mares."

"But it is my fault, I'm afraid."

"What?"

"You see, I fetched some rubbish from Tibbett's with the tractor this afternoon, and I must have left the gate open. That's how some of the ponies ended up in Middle Park. The gate's still open. I'm so sorry!"

Jenny looked at Ben's red face staring down at her, and burst out laughing. She lay on the heather and laughed helplessly, so her aching sides ached even more. "Don't worry. I had the ride of my life!" she managed to say. "He's like Pegasus – we flew!"

With a sigh of relief, Ben plonked himself down on the ground beside Jenny. He was laughing too.

They laughed so much that tears streamed down their faces. Eventually they lay exhausted, staring up at the grey sky. A thin drizzle drifted by on the breeze.

"I suppose we'd better get those ponies back where they belong," said Jenny. She felt so incredibly weak that even talking was an effort. "You won't tell anybody about this, will you?"

"No, of course not." Ben jumped up, and held out his hand.

Jenny took it, and he pulled her up. As she fell towards him, he gave her a quick hug. "I'm so glad you're okay," he said.

They parted, slightly embarrassed, and went to put the ponies back where they belonged.

8

The rest of the summer whizzed by. The weather was good, so Lundy was heaving with visitors. Work got in the way constantly, and left very little spare time for Jenny to spend with Midnight or Ben.

All too soon, it was Ben's last day on the island.

Jenny knew she'd miss him terribly. There would be no possibility of meeting him somewhere by chance, or going swimming before breakfast – or anytime, come to that – and there would be nobody to help her with Midnight and share in her triumphs and disasters. Lundy would be a lonely place without him.

It was a mark of how much everyone liked Ben that

they organised a leaving party for him. They'd all miss his cheerful, easy-going nature. He was a good worker and didn't mind what he did. He fitted in.

The leaving party followed the familiar and well-loved pattern of parties in the Tavern, with food, drink and plenty of homemade entertainment.

As everyone finished their plates of food, Mr Hamilton got up and rapped the table for silence.

"Watch out! Speech time!" Jenny whispered to Ben. Ben made a face.

Mr Hamilton smiled at his audience. He thoroughly enjoyed making speeches. "A few months ago, Albert approached me to enquire about a summer job for young Ben here. I considered . . ."

The respectful silence of the audience was broken as Gareth, PK of the North Light, burst into the Tavern. The door slammed behind him, stopping Mr Hamilton in mid-sentence.

"That damned stallion! He tried to kill me, I swear it!" Gareth exclaimed. "I was walking along, minding my own business, and he came at me out of the blue! Galloping straight at me, he was – scared me to death! He ought to be shot!"

Mr Hamilton's speech was forgotten. A crowd gathered round Gareth, eager to hear more.

Jenny's happiness evaporated. The room suddenly felt horribly crowded. She had to get out. "I'm sorry,

Ben. I've got to go. I need some fresh air," she shouted in his ear. "Have a good time. I'll see you tomorrow."

The night was clear and bathed in silvery moonlight, like it had been on Jenny's birthday, but not so warm. The air felt thinner and tasted of autumn. Jenny gulped it in, like a drowning fish. The fun of the party seemed a distant memory. Midnight was in serious trouble, and she didn't know what to do.

"Everything's gone wrong!" she wailed to the starlit sky as she hurried up the High Street and past her cottage.

She heard footsteps running up behind her. "I'm so sorry, Jenny! It's my fault, isn't it? I was the one who suggested giving him sugar lumps, and now he chases after people, hoping they've got some. It must be that, mustn't it?" Ben caught up with her, and took hold of her arm. "Where are you going?"

"I'm going to see Midnight."

"But . . . Oh, all right. I'll come with you."

"You can't. You'll miss your party."

"My party's finished. It seems to be Gareth's party now."

They walked on in companionable silence, disturbing some ewes resting by the path. Their shoes squashed sheep droppings between the crunchy granite gravel underfoot, and left a strong, musty smell hanging in the still, damp air.

As they approached Pondsbury, they heard the dull thud of hooves. Midnight came cantering towards them, leaping over tussocks of gorse and heather in his way, kicking up sprays of silvery dew-drops. He looked like a mythical creature in the moonlight.

"Oh, he's so beautiful!" Jenny whispered. "A storybook horse."

"Fairy tale, or horror story?"

Jenny sighed. "That's the trouble – he's a bit of both, isn't he?"

"Perhaps we should rename him Nightmare," Ben said.

"Oh! That's unfair! Poor Midnight!"

The stallion trotted up, ears pricked, eager for a treat. He nuzzled at Jenny's pockets.

"Sorry, old boy. No more sugar from now on. You're getting spoilt," Jenny said, pushing him away firmly as he tried to nip her pocket.

He turned to Ben, hoping for better luck, but Ben pushed him away as well. Put out, Midnight turned away and stood with his ears back, swishing his tail sulkily. Jenny walked round to his head, rubbed his neck and talked to him. He blew gently through his nose and rested a hind leg. His eyelids drooped and his lips trembled.

Jenny smiled to herself. "There! You see? This is much better than sugar, isn't it?" she said softly. "You're not to go chasing people again. They don't know you're just looking for food; they think you're attacking them. You can come up to me, but no one else. Understand? Now I'd better go, because it's Ben's last night."

Ben walked up to join her at Midnight's side. "It's okay, I'm quite happy stargazing," he said.

"Do you know what they're all called?" Jenny asked, looking up at the sky.

"Not all of them, but I know some. Dad taught me. Look, I'll show you." Ben stood behind Jenny, and pointed northwards over her shoulder. She could feel the warmth of his body against her back. "See those seven bright stars in the shape of a saucepan? That's the Plough, a part of Ursa Major, or the Great Bear."

"Oh, yes!" Jenny exclaimed.

"Now then," Ben continued, tracing a line in the sky with his finger while holding her hand in his. "Go on in a straight line from the lip of the saucepan, and you'll see the North Star, Polaris. It's the bright one – there. That's attached to a smaller saucepan, which is Ursa Minor, the Little Bear."

It's all so clear, once it's pointed out, Jenny thought. I must try to remember all this.

"Now then, if you pretend the big saucepan, Ursa

Major, has a hole, and its contents have spilled out of the bottom of the pan, that's Leo. See? It's supposed to look like a lion."

"That's my star sign!" Jenny said.

"Well, there you are, then. You now know how to find your own stars."

"That star in the middle's much brighter than the rest, isn't it, Ben?"

"Yes, that's Regulus, the lion's heart."

Midnight stood with his head over Jenny's left shoulder. He seemed to be looking at the stars too.

"When I'm away on the mainland, Midnight, you can look at that star and think of me, and I'll look at that star and think of you," Jenny said. She turned to stroke the stallion's neck, and looked eastwards to the distant dark strip of land beyond the sea, dotted with pin-prick lights.

At that moment, the mainland seemed as far away as the stars. She wished it could stay that way forever.

Jenny stood at a lookout point above the bay, squinting into the distance as the boat, with Ben on board, disappeared from view. It was mid-afternoon, and she didn't know what to do. Normally she'd have been down on the beach, swimming and climbing rocks, or trying to hitch a ride with one of the fishermen.

Now nothing seemed worth doing. She ached with loneliness, but couldn't bear the thought of company.

There's one more week to go, then I'll be leaving for the mainland too, Jenny thought miserably. The previously distant dread of school suddenly seemed very real and unavoidable – like heading for a wall on a galloping horse.

The sound of a child's voice interrupted her gloomy thoughts. "Jenny?"

She sighed as she saw Camilla standing on the path below. "Yes?"

"Have you seen Hector? He's stolen my sweets and I can't find him *anywhere!*" Camilla lisped through her gappy teeth.

Jenny really didn't want to get involved, although she felt sorry for Camilla. Hector was so mean to her sometimes. "No, I'm afraid I haven't seen anyone," she replied.

"Oh. Can you help me find him?"

"I'm afraid not. I've got to go and cook Dad's supper," Jenny said. Well, it's much kinder than saying I want to be left alone, she thought.

Camilla looked crestfallen.

Jenny felt guilty. "Tell you what," she said, "I'll look for Hector on my way home."

"Thanks!" Camilla said, and she ran back down the path to Millcombe.

Jenny walked slowly towards the village. Dapples of light shone through the leafy branches overhead. She couldn't face going home yet, so she veered right and took the path along the East Sidelands. After a while she found a flat rock where she could sit down. There's nothing to look forward to any more, only things to dread, she thought as she stared out to sea. The mainland was a solid blue-grey strip on the skyline, and the water shimmered in the early evening sun. Ben would be on the home stretch by now, if he still thought of it as home. He'd told her last night that he'd never felt as much at home anywhere as he had on Lundy.

"I really love Lundy," he'd said. "You're so lucky to live here."

Remembering his words made Jenny feel even more depressed. She wasn't going to be living here for much longer either. With the whole summer before her, school hadn't seemed real. It was all too real now. She felt like a trapped animal, and wondered why she'd ever agreed to it. She didn't need riding lessons *that* badly. Perhaps it wasn't too late to change her mind. Dad had said he wouldn't make her go, after all. But everything had been arranged – even her school uniform, which was going to be ready and waiting when she arrived on the mainland. She couldn't back out now, could she? What about Midnight, though? What would happen to him? How could she go to school when his future on the island hung in the balance? No, she thought. I can't go to school, and that's final. We'll be able to send the uniform back, I'm sure. I'll go home and tell Dad now.

Her spirits soared as she got up and started running towards home. She'd stay at home with Dad. Nothing would change. She felt as free as a bird.

Just before the old ruins of Quarter Wall Cottages, Jenny saw Mr Bonham approaching along the path, carrying Hector in his arms. She stepped to one side and smiled as they passed by, but Mr Bonham just nodded briefly in return. The expression on his face was unusually grim. Hector was sobbing.

Good, thought Jenny. I hope he's found out he can't steal sweets from Camilla and get away with it.

Jenny burst through the front door of her cottage, her speech about not wanting to go to school fully formed and ready to be delivered.

It was only a moment, but she saw it clearly. Dad and Sheila were hugging each other in the kitchen! They pulled apart quickly.

Dad looked flustered. "Ah, Jenny!" he said in an unusually hearty sort of voice. "Sheila's just dropped by with a pie for our supper, isn't that kind of her?"

Jenny couldn't think of anything to say.

"Oh, and guess what arrived in the mail today?" He

lifted a large white envelope from the kitchen table, and handed it to her. "A letter from your Housemistress telling you how much they're looking forward to seeing you next week. And you'll be glad to know I've paid in advance for piano and riding lessons, so you've got nothing to worry about – it's all sorted."

Defeated, Jenny took the envelope from Dad's outstretched hand, went into her bedroom and shut the door.

9

The countdown to school had begun. Two days
sped by, and then it was Tuesday. The weather was
damp and there was a day-trip of depressed-looking
visitors.

Jenny had to help in the kitchen. Sheila was her
usually chatty self, but Jenny gave short, reluctant
answers to her frequent questions. Jenny couldn't give
a name to how she felt. It was more complicated than
hatred or anger. Resentment? Jealousy? Whatever it
was, everything about Sheila had become irritating.
She found it hard to look at her, speak to her or be
anywhere near her. Eventually an awkward silence
prevailed. Afterwards, Jenny wondered whether she'd

have found out who was staying in the Hotel that night if she'd been more talkative.

When Jenny woke on Wednesday morning, it was raining hard.

"I'll do the animals, if you like. No need for both of us to get wet. There's something I've got to do this morning, but I should be back by lunch time," Dad said when he brought Jenny an early morning cup of tea. "Why don't you have a quiet time inside? Recharge your batteries a bit, read a book or something. After all, you won't be able to be a bookworm for much longer – you'll be having too much fun."

Jenny wanted to scream or throw something at him when he reminded her of school like that, but she just kept quiet and shrivelled inside. She couldn't deny that she was dying to read the rest of her book, though. It was so good that for a while she forgot her worries . . .

The story ended, and thoughts of school, Midnight, Dad and Sheila instantly filled the void. She searched for something else to read, and found the book Albert had given her for her birthday. It was called *The Little Prince*, and it had become lost under a pile of clothes on the floor. On the cover there was a picture of a boy standing on a tiny planet surrounded by stars; he looked like a small version of Ben, complete with an untidy mop of fair hair. Jenny started to read, hoping to become lost in another story, but the illustrations kept reminding her of Ben, which made her think of the mainland, and school, and all her other worries. In despair, she decided to go for a walk. Out of her bedroom window she could see that it had stopped raining and the sky was looking lighter. She'd go and see Midnight and Gale.

A s soon as Jenny left the cottage, she could hear shouting and banging from the shippen yard. Something squealed. A pig? It sounded more forceful than a pig.

A shiver of dread ran through her. She hurried towards the yard, more certain with every step that her fears would be confirmed.

Several men stood in a wide semi-circle around a plunging, terrified horse. Jenny saw, to her horror, that the horse was Midnight.

The men waved their arms and shouted a lot, trying to drive him forwards. Midnight wrestled madly against a rope around his neck. A man stood in front of him, holding the long tail of the rope, keeping up the pressure. Jenny recognised him as Dave Dobson, who'd been given the jokey nickname of Dobbin by the islanders.

Dobbin lived on the mainland, where he broke, bought and sold horses. For some reason he'd become the island's pony agent and all-round expert. Jenny couldn't understand it. He gave her the creeps, and he was horribly rough with the ponies. One day she'd asked her dad why they'd chosen Dobbin, of all people, to deal with the ponies.

"He's been doing it for years, and he's the only person I know who's daft enough to want to do it," Dad had replied. "It's one hell of a job to catch an unhandled pony, drag it down to the beach, swim it out to the boat, load it, take it to the mainland and sell it. I wouldn't want to, would you?"

Jenny had admitted she wouldn't.

"He always gets the job done, one way or the other, and that's the main thing," Dad had added.

Jenny couldn't agree with that. Didn't being kind count as a main thing? Sometimes she didn't understand her father at all.

Midnight braced against the rope, rearing, slithering and grunting in a surge of effort. Someone hit him on the rump, and he plunged forward.

Dobbin took up the slack.

"Midnight! Oh, no! Stop! Stop it!" Jenny screamed, climbing over the yard gate and running towards Dobbin. "Stop it! Let him go!"

"Keep away. You could get hurt," Dobbin said gruffly.

"*He's* the one getting hurt! What are you trying to do? Let him go!"

Dad came over. "That's enough, Jenny. I'm sorry. You weren't supposed to see this, but it's for his own good. Dobbin, er, Mr Dobson, knows what he's doing. We're just trying to get Midnight into a shed so we can get a head collar on him and take him down to the boat. He's going to have a nice new home on the mainland. You go home now, and I'll be along in a minute," he said.

Sweat dripped from Midnight's flanks, and his stiffened legs trembled with fear. Dark red blood oozed from a gash on his knee. His wide, wild eyes studied everyone intently, waiting for their next move, ready to fight again.

All of a sudden, Jenny knew how she could save him – or at least give him the chance to save himself. "No, I'm staying," she said. "Midnight knows me. I'll help."

"Jenny, I really don't see how you can help, and I don't want you getting hurt. Leave it to Mr Dobson. He's the expert."

Before anyone could stop her, Jenny approached Midnight gently. She started stroking him, talking softly all the time.

He flinched away from her to begin with, but soon relaxed enough for her to feel confident about trying the next stage of her plan.

"Can you let go of the rope, please?" she asked Dobbin.

He glowered at Jenny, but did as she asked.

"Please stand back, everyone, so you don't scare him." Jenny said as she gathered up the rope. Then she took a deep breath to calm herself, and headed for the double doors of the shippen. Midnight followed obediently.

"Hold hard! We were going to put him in the smaller shed," Dobbin said.

"Oh, but there's much more room in the shippen, and it's not so dark. He's more likely to go in there without a fuss," Jenny replied.

"Okay, makes no odds," Dobbin muttered.

After a moment's hesitation, Midnight followed Jenny inside. She slipped the rope over his neck. "It's up to you now," she whispered. "Good luck!" Then she left, slamming the doors hard and bolting them behind her, hoping the noise would spur Midnight into action.

The men burst into spontaneous applause. Dobbin joined in half-heartedly. The sound of clapping was replaced by a crashing, scraping sound. Everyone looked alarmed. Jenny tried not to smile.

Dobbin rushed to the shippen, pulled back the rusty bolts, opened the top door and looked inside. He swore loudly, flung the bottom door open and ran in. More swear words.

They all piled into the shippen to see for themselves. The back wall had several stones missing, and Midnight had gone. They were just in time to catch a glimpse of him jumping from the ducks' pen into Tent Field. Then, with a flick of his tail, he disappeared from view.

Jenny had never seen her father so angry. He paced round the kitchen, shaking with rage and spluttering out words like an erupting volcano.

"You *idiot!* All that effort! We had him! At long last, we had him! But *you* let him go! *Deliberately* let him go!" He paused for breath, trying to calm down. "It's all so clear now! That's what happened the last time, wasn't it? When the mare and foal were in there? You had Midnight in there as well, but he escaped, didn't he? You put him in there today hoping he'd escape again, didn't you? *Didn't you?*"

"Yes," Jenny whispered.

"You silly, selfish girl! You didn't even *think* to ask *why* we were catching him, did you? Oh no! You just thought you'd take the law into your own hands! This isn't some ridiculous pony story about wild stallions, gymkhanas and happily-ever-after rubbish, you know. This is *real life!*" Dad stood still. Leaning on the table with both hands, he looked straight into her eyes. "Real life is messy and complicated, and things never turn out as they should," he said emphatically. "Try this for a real life story: on Saturday evening, Mr

Bonham found Midnight attacking Hector near the Quarry Cottages. He was after Hector's bag of sweets, apparently. The poor little boy was terrified; who knows what might have happened if he hadn't been found in time? Understandably, Mr Bonham wanted the stallion destroyed. However, knowing how fond you are of Midnight, I asked if he could be sent to the mainland instead. Mr Bonham very generously agreed, organised the boat and paid for Dobbin to come over. All went well. The sea was calm, we managed to catch Midnight, and it looked as if he'd be in a cosy stable on the mainland by nightfall. But then you came along – and I think you can fill in the rest, can't you, Jenny?"

Jenny felt weak with the full realisation of what she'd done.

"So now," Dad continued, "there isn't a hope in hell of catching him before the boat goes in an hour or two, and I'll have to go and shoot him later on, when everything's calmed down a bit. I'm sorry to be so brutal, Jenny, but that's the reality."

Jenny fled into her room and flung herself onto her bed, wailing in anguish, gulping for air, drowning in grief. Her agony for Midnight was mixed with anger at herself for making things worse by trying to tame him, setting him free in the shippen, not trying to find Hector when Camilla had asked her to . . .

She sensed her father had come into the room.

"Jenny?" His voice wasn't angry any more, just sad. "I'm sorry, love. Truly I am."

"Go away! I hate you!"

She heard her bedroom door click shut, and then the sound of Dad washing up. After a while, the noise from the kitchen changed. The radio crackled into life, and there were intermittent thumping, scraping and clattering noises. It sounded as if some serious cleaning was going on.

Jenny rolled over and sat up on the side of her bed, occasionally shuddering with yet another heart-wrenching sob. She longed for her father's strong, reassuring arms round her, but she couldn't face him. She was stuck in her room, and couldn't think what to do. The book she'd been reading earlier lay on the floor beside her bed. She sighed and picked it up, struck again by how the pictures of the Little Prince looked like Ben. Flicking through the pages, she found where she thought she'd stopped reading the last time, and tried to read some more. Again, she could barely concentrate, and she was just about to give up when a passage in the book fought its way through all the turmoil and lodged in her mind. Stunned, she read and re-read it. A fox was asking the Little Prince to tame him, so they could become friends. The fox said that the Little Prince would have to be patient and quiet, and sit a little closer every day – just as Jenny had done with Midnight. What's more, he said that if you tame a wild animal, the course of its life changes forever and you become responsible for its future.

"I can't let Midnight die!" Jenny said to herself. "I've tamed him, so I'm responsible for him. I've got to save him!"

She rummaged around in her drawer for the rope halter and some sugar lumps.

Her coat hung on the back of the door. Trying to make as little noise as possible, she put it on, filled the pockets with sugar lumps, opened her bedroom window and climbed out.

She sprinted up the track towards Quarter Wall, repeating under her breath, "Please let me find him in time! Please let everything be all right!"

10

Somehow, Jenny knew the ponies would be down by the quarries. Her heart hammered in her chest when she saw them, but she forced herself to calm down. She knew Midnight wouldn't allow himself to be caught if he sensed her nerves. This was her one and only chance to put things right. If she failed Midnight would die, she was sure of that. Her father wouldn't lie about something so serious, and he was an excellent shot. He never missed a rabbit, and Midnight would be a much easier target than a rabbit. She shuddered at the thought.

Midnight walked away as she approached him. For a moment she was terrified he'd run. She put the halter down, and took some sugar lumps out of her pocket.

He turned to face her, wary but interested.

Jenny put a sugar lump in her mouth and sucked it, hoping it would lure him in. She ate a few more, realising she hadn't eaten anything since breakfast.

Midnight pawed the ground uncertainly and kept his distance, but Gale hurried over. She'd grown into a stocky, rather scruffy little filly. A sandy-coloured winter coat grew unevenly between her creamy baby hair, and her legs were blotchy as they turned from light to dark.

"Hello, gorgeous. Want a sweetie?"

Gale crunched a sugar lump happily, then nudged Jenny for more. Jenny stroked her and talked to her, and gave her an occasional titbit. Every second counted, but she had to pretend she had all the time in the world.

Eventually, Midnight walked up and pinned his ears back at Gale, warning her off. Then he pricked his ears forward, giving Jenny an innocent, pleading look.

From devil to angel in less than a second, Jenny thought. She gave him a sugar lump, and another, and another. His guard dropped, and he allowed her to slip the halter over his head while he munched. Then, feeding him sugar lumps at regular intervals, she led him along the track, past the Timekeeper's Hut, round the edge of Quarry Pond, up the hill and over to the

Quarter Wall gate. The mares and foals followed at a respectful distance, with Rosie in the lead.

Midnight was concentrating so hard on the contents of Jenny's pockets that it was only when they had nearly reached Barton Cottages, and the mares shut behind the Quarter Wall gate had started calling, that he noticed he'd left the herd behind. Instantly agitated, he whinnied loudly and tried to rear.

Jenny fed him a handful of sugar lumps, and kept walking.

He tossed his head, spraying her with sugary froth from his mouth. Then he plunged forwards, squealing and whinnying in the same breath.

A searing pain burned into her hands as the rope dragged through them, but she hung on and jerked with all her might on it. "Stop that! Behave!" she shouted. Her hands stung even more, and her eyes blurred with tears.

Midnight, obviously astonished, wheeled round and stood still. He looked magnificent: ears pricked, eyes flashing, neck arched, tail high and every muscle in his body taut with anticipation. Ready to explode into action. Terrifying.

Jenny gave him yet another sugar lump. It had red blotches on it from her bleeding hand, but he didn't seem to notice. His sugary saliva stung her palm. Ignoring the pain, she reached inside her pocket for more sugar. There were only a couple of lumps left.

It's hopeless! I won't be able to get him to the yard, let alone down to the Landing Beach, she thought desperately.

Without warning Midnight spooked at something behind him. He wheeled round, knocking Jenny sideways. She knew she'd lose him for good if she fell over, so somehow she stayed upright and clung on to the rope.

"Jenny! What on *earth?* I thought you were in bed!"

"Careful, Dad! You'll frighten him. Keep back," Jenny said quickly. "I'm almost out of sugar lumps. Can you get some? They're under my pants."

"What?"

"Sugar lumps, in my bedroom. There's a box in the top drawer, under my pants." Jenny managed to sound much calmer than she felt. "Please hurry."

After what seemed like ages, Dad came back. He approached Jenny carefully, and filled her pockets with the remaining sugar lumps from the box.

"Thanks, Dad," she said quietly, offering Midnight several in one go. "Somehow, I've got to keep his mind off the mares and get him down to the boat."

"I'll walk behind, and we'll take it one step at a time," he replied, smiling at her reassuringly. She had an overwhelming urge to hug him.

All went well until they neared the Tavern, where

Dobbin and his helpers had decided to pass the time until the tide was right for the boat to leave. Someone must have spotted Jenny and Midnight, because suddenly everyone crowded out of the Tavern, whistling, cheering and clapping.

Midnight stopped, petrified, eyes bulging.

At any moment he'll bolt, Jenny thought. She held the rope tightly, trying to ignore the stinging pain in her hands. The grand entry of her dreams, with Midnight perfectly under control, wasn't turning out quite as she'd planned.

"Quiet!" Dobbin yelled above the din.

The noise subsided to an excited murmur.

"Right then," Dobbin said, taking charge. "Just stay there for a moment, there's a good girl. Don't let go, now. I'll get a proper headcollar and take over from here. You'll never be able to hold him going down the Beach Road."

Someone handed Dobbin his special headcollar, which had a chain running through it for extra control. He approached confidently, clicking his tongue softly against his teeth. "There's a good boy," he coaxed. His eyes narrowed in concentration and his body tensed, like a cat ready to pounce.

Midnight sensed it, and shied away, yanking the rope through Jenny's raw hands. She gasped with pain. "Please don't! You're upsetting him. I'll manage."

"Suddenly you're the horse expert, are you?" Dobbin sneered. "Give him to me." He grabbed hold of the rope.

Midnight struck out with a forefoot, hitting Dobbin's leg so hard that he reeled backwards in agony.

"Why, you little beggar! Just you wait!" he hissed, nursing his leg and his wounded pride. His hard eyes focused on Jenny. "Okay, you take him, then. But don't you dare let go!" He walked back to the crowd, trying to conceal a limp. "He's used to the girl, so it's best if she takes him," he said. "James, walk in front with me. We'll stop him if he tries to makes a dash for it."

Jenny secretly doubted whether a hundred people would be able to stop Midnight if he made a dash for it. "The rest of you, walk behind with Robert. Go steady, and don't get too close. That pony's got a kick like a mule."

Jenny offered Midnight a few sugar lumps, but he wasn't interested in them any more. She walked forwards again, praying he'd follow.

She needn't have worried. He followed her willingly, wary of all the people around him, seeking her protection. The lead rope hung loosely as he walked with his head near her shoulder, as if tied by an invisible thread. He believes I'll look after him, she thought. Silent tears trickled down her cheeks as she walked down the Beach Road to the waiting boat.

The sea looked oily-calm. At least the crossing wouldn't be rough.

"We'll take over now," Dobbin said once they reached the Landing Beach. He held a large canvas sling with a pole running through it. Several buckles and a rope attached to a ring hung from it, swinging and clanking.

Midnight pushed into Jenny, seeking reassurance.

"It's okay. They're not going to hurt you," Jenny soothed, stroking his neck. He knows I'm lying, she thought. Her hands shook.

"Hold this, Robert. We'd better tie him first," said Dobbin, handing Dad the sling so he could unravel a piece of rope which had been coiled over his shoulder. "James, come and take the lead rope."

"It's okay, I'll be fine," Jenny said. "I want to stay with him."

"This is no place for a girl. Let James have him now," Dobbin said firmly.

"No! He needs me!"

"Do as you're told! You've caused us enough trouble already," Dobbin barked.

"There's no call for that sort of talk. Come on, Jenny, you've done your bit. I'll take you home," Dad said kindly.

James took the rope from Jenny.

She stroked Midnight's trembling neck. "Good luck," she whispered. Through a blur of tears she caught a glimpse of a blue eye, wide and frightened. As she walked away, Midnight tried to follow.

"Oh, no you don't, you brute!" James said, jerking the lead rope.

"Hold him steady, and I'll tie him so he doesn't kick us while we put the sling on," she heard Dobbin say. Then she heard the crashing of shingle as Midnight tried to break free, and a thud as he fell over. Swearing and shouting from the men. Terrified, outraged grunting and squealing from Midnight. More crashing.

Jenny heard, but she dared not look. Even if everything went according to plan, she knew the journey ahead would be terrible for Midnight. With the sling secured round his stomach, he would be attached by a rope to a rowing boat with three men in it. Another rope would run from the rowing boat to the larger boat out in the bay. The men at the front would pull the rowing boat towards the larger boat, and the man at the back would hang on to Midnight's head to stop him from drowning. Then, on reaching the big boat, Midnight's sling would be attached to a system of ropes and pulleys on the boat, and he'd be winched into the hold, which was a small, stuffy place below the deck. If the boat made it to the mainland before Midnight wrecked it, he'd have to be winched ashore and transported by lorry to Dobbin's yard.

Jenny knew lots of ponies and cattle made a similar tortuous journey every year – it was the only way to get them off Lundy so they could be sold – but that wasn't any consolation. I shouldn't have caught him, she thought miserably. He'd have been better off dead on Lundy.

She trudged up the Beach Road, grateful for her father's strong, protective arm around her shoulders. "What'll happen to him?" she asked after a while.

"He'll be fine, don't you worry. Mr Dobson will look after him and train him, and then he'll sell him on to a good home."

"Where will he sell him?"

"I don't know, Jenny love. The autumn horse sale in Barnstaple is where he usually sells the ponies."

"How can you be sure he'll go to a good home if he's going to be sold at market? He may go for, for d-dog f-food." Jenny stammered. The tears welled up again.

That night, Jenny couldn't sleep. She put some jeans and a jumper on over her pyjamas, and climbed out of her bedroom window.

Stars sparkled in the ink-black sky.

Had Midnight arrived safely? She wouldn't know until Mr Hamilton made his morning radio call to the

Hartland Coastguard. There was nothing she could do but wait. She searched the sky and found the Plough, then Leo the lion, and then Regulus, the lion's heart.

"I'm so sorry, Midnight," she said. "You trusted me, and I betrayed you. I don't know how yet, but I'm going to make everything all right when I get to the mainland. I won't let you down again, I promise."

PART II

Another World

11

The boat heaved through the lumpy waves and belched diesel fumes over the deck. Shivering uncontrollably, Jenny groaned, hung her head over the side and was sick yet again. In the brief period afterwards, when she felt well enough to think of anything other than survival, panic gripped her. In a few hours she'd be at St Anne's School for Girls. It was utterly impossible.

All around, the dark metallic sea merged with heavy low clouds. Lundy, in one direction, and the North Devon coast, in the other, were somewhere behind the grey shroud, but she had no idea where. She was in a violent, liquid no-man's-land. The only indication that the boat was on course came from a strong south-westerly wind, which buffeted her and blew her hair in front of her face.

Bang! A wave smashed into the boat head-on, sending a cascade of spray into the air. The prow reared and then dropped into the void left by the passing wave. *Crash!* The boat quivered, rose and plunged again, boring through endless troughs and peaks in the turbulent sea.

She gripped the side of the boat and retched on a cramped, empty stomach. It felt as if she were being turned inside-out.

Jenny glanced over at Mrs Hamilton. She didn't look well, either.

A strong hand rested briefly on her shoulder.

"Why don't you come into the cabin, Jenny? It's warmer in there," said Captain Dover.

She nodded in reply. Mrs Hamilton's advice that the deck was always the best place to be if you felt sick didn't seem right; a warm cabin sounded much better.

The boat teetered, fell and wallowed, heeled, swayed and rocked, but Captain Dover walked along the deck as if he were taking a stroll up the High Street. Jenny tried to follow as best she could, lurching shakily from one handhold to the next until she reached the sanctuary of the small cabin.

"Lie here, maid. It's always better if you lie down,"

said the Captain, pointing to a short wooden bench. "You can use this jersey as a cushion, if you like."

The jersey was chunky and rough. It smelled of stale tobacco, engine oil and fish, but Jenny was past caring. It was a shred of soft comfort in the hard, wet, cold world she'd been plunged into. She sank onto the bench and curled up on her side, with the jersey scrunched into a makeshift pillow under her head.

Lunging and creaking, the boat juddered on. Jenny braced herself as she was flung inwards, and then her back bumped against the cabin wall as she was flung outwards. Brace, bump, brace, bump, brace, bump – her body rocked to and fro as the waves rolled and crashed.

There was another man in the cabin. He seemed unbelievably relaxed. Captain Dover took over the helm, and the two men talked and joked. Their low voices rose and fell against the noise of the engine.

Jenny closed her eyes. Perhaps, against all odds, I'll survive the journey. Perhaps I'll see Ben, and we'll rescue Midnight somehow. Perhaps school will be okay after all . . . The men's voices faded into a distant corner of her mind.

Jenny woke, certain she was going to be sick. She had that unmistakable tingling feeling as her mouth filled with saliva. Through her half-opened eyes she could see Captain Dover smoking a pipe with great enthusiasm, filling the cabin with thick, pungent smoke. The other man had left the cabin.

Before she could get up, Jenny was sick. She was sick on her hair and on the jersey she'd been using as a pillow. It was so awful that for a brief moment she considered running out on deck and jumping overboard. Instead, she just sat there and stared in disbelief as the slimy bile seeped into the wool.

"I am *so* sorry," she whispered, not daring to look up.

"Ha! Don't you worry!" Captain Dover said heartily. "It's due for a wash. It's had worse things on it, I can tell you."

Jenny wondered what on earth could be worse than sick.

"Here, you'd better clean yourself up. We're coming into Bideford," Captain Dover said, handing her an oil-stained towel which didn't smell much cleaner than the jersey. "You're in good company," he added, winking.

Mrs Hamilton came into the cabin. She looked different – sort of blue and unusually ruffled, but also different in her face. Her mouth was pinched and wrinkled, and her speech was slurred.

Until then, Jenny had never thought of teeth as

being important for anything other than eating. Mrs Hamilton must have lost her false teeth overboard when she was sick. How on earth could she take Jenny to school now? It would be *so* embarrassing!

Captain Dover handed a small box to Mrs Hamilton. "Put your dentures back in, Peggy. Here's Bideford." He turned to Jenny and said in a stage whisper, "She was queasy a few years back, and parted company with her gnashers, so now I keep them safe for her if we're in for a bumpy ride."

Usually Jenny would have laughed, but all she managed was a wan smile of relief. Through the misty cabin window she could see the solid grey outline of a large, unfamiliar coastline dotted with buildings. She felt panic tingling through her body and grabbing at her heart. The boat, which had seemed like hell on earth an hour ago, was now a safe haven. It was her link with Lundy. She didn't want to leave it and embark on the most daunting journey of her life: the journey to boarding school.

12

As soon as Jenny stepped off the boat onto Bideford Quay, she felt like an alien in a chaotic, overpopulated foreign country. The only comfort was that the inhabitants spoke the same language, more or less.

In contrast, Mrs Hamilton seemed excited and very much at home. A trip to the mainland for a couple of days was a rare treat, and it was clear she intended to enjoy every minute of it.

"Let's go to my hotel and get changed. Then we'll have a spot of lunch and take a taxi to St Anne's. How does that sound?"

Fine, except for the last bit, Jenny thought. "Fine,"

she said, making a brave attempt at a smile.

Jenny felt chilled to her core. She sank gratefully into the huge hotel bath. Even tepid water made her skin sting, but as she thawed out she topped up the bath with more hot, clear water from the impressive brass mixer tap which gurgled and gushed. Soon the bath was full enough to overflow.

The water on Lundy was always peaty-brown and in short supply. This was luxury.

The hotel soap smelled like a summer garden. She washed her body and her hair, and then allowed herself several minutes of pure indulgence – not thinking, just feeling. She drifted about, soaking in warmth, blocking out all thoughts of what was to come . . .

Knock! Knock! "Jenny? Are you all right in there?" Mrs Hamilton's voice made her jump.

She scrambled out of the bath, spilling water onto the bathmat and surrounding floor. "Yes, thanks! Coming!"

The bath towels were white, thick and soft. Jenny wrapped one round her, and tried to empty the bath. After several futile attempts at pulling out a shiny metal disc, which appeared to be the bath plug, she managed to make it pop up by pulling a lever below the tap. Fascinating! She did it several times, for fun.

"Jenny?"

"Just coming!"

"So is Christmas."

Reluctantly, Jenny emerged from the steaming bathroom: bright red, squeaky clean and cocooned in a massive towel.

"How very apt!" Mrs Hamilton exclaimed, smiling. "You look like a chrysalis, ready to transform into a butterfly! I've hung your school uniform on the back of the door, and there's a hairdryer over there on the dressing table. You get ready, while I have a quick bath." She disappeared into the bathroom, and shut the door.

Jenny heard the gurgle and gush of the bath tap. Gingerly, she took down her uniform and put it on, piece by uncomfortable piece.

The starched white shirt felt crisply cold against her warm body. The long navy blue woollen socks were itchy and too big. They kept trying to fall down.

Likewise, the pleated blue tartan kilt-skirt was too big in all directions. It hung loosely on her hips, rather than at her waist, so that the hem nearly reached her ankles.

At least the blazer hid everything else. It dwarfed her, hanging shapelessly from her narrow shoulders and finishing just below her bottom.

Surely I can't have lost that much weight on the boat trip this morning! Jenny thought, despairing at her image in the mirror. She put her blue-and-grey-striped tie round her neck, pushed it under the stiff shirt collar and attempted to tie it. The harder she tried, the worse it turned out. She had another go, and another.

Mrs Hamilton emerged from the bathroom, dressed in a tweed skirt, twin-set and pearls. "Well, what a transformation! You do look smart!"

Jenny rounded on her, courageous in her despair. "No I don't! It's all far too big! Hideous! I can't have shrunk *that* much since you measured me in the summer!"

Unphased, Mrs Hamilton said, "I ordered a size larger, to give room for growth. Girls your age do grow tremendously quickly; you wait and see. Come here, and I'll show you how to tie your tie."

Jenny found Mrs Hamilton's ability to ward off rebellion infuriating, but rather reassuring at the same time.

As Mrs Hamilton placed the tie around Jenny's neck, the familiar smell of her scented talcum powder wafted in the air. "This is by far the easiest method, and quite adequate for school," she said. "Mr Hamilton would be appalled, of course; he likes a Windsor knot, but that's rather more complicated. He always says you can tell a gentleman by the way he knots his tie. Now then, watch how I do it." With a few deft movements, she tied a perfect knot. "There! Bob's your uncle. Now you try."

After several attempts Jenny mastered it, and wondered why she'd found it so difficult.

"Jolly good! That's that, then. You do look smart!

Shoes on. Time for lunch," said Mrs Hamilton.

The shoes were shiny, stiff and at least a size too big. They made a flapping noise as Jenny walked cautiously down the stairs.

She felt light-headed with hunger at the intense smell of hot food which greeted them as they walked into the plush, stuffy dining room. The tables had spotless white tablecloths. They were laid with stiff white linen table napkins folded into fans, a spectacular array of silver cutlery, and sparkling glasses of various shapes and sizes. The chairs had ornate frames and deep purple upholstery. Jenny felt out of place as she followed Mrs Hamilton to their table, weaving between some seated diners, with her eyes fixed on the carpet to avoid looking at anyone. The carpet was also deep purple, with elaborate gold swirls which made her rather dizzy.

A waiter held out her chair and called her "young lady". The hot, airless room began to turn, leaving her behind. This is all a weird dream. I'll wake up on Lundy in a minute, she thought . . .

"Mum?" Jenny murmured. "Mummy, is that you?" Through a haze of semi-consciousness she saw the most beautiful face looking tenderly at her, and felt her hand being stroked gently. I must have died and gone to heaven, she thought.

"No, dear. I'm not your mother. You fainted, but you'll be fine. Lie still for a minute or two, and then we'll get you onto a chair. Your mother's just here."

"I'm afraid her mother is no longer with us. I'm her guardian," said Mrs Hamilton.

"Oh, I'm so sorry. I didn't realise."

Fully conscious now, Jenny was overwhelmed with embarrassment. She lay on the swirly carpet, surrounded by cutlery, broken glass and table linen, and stared in dismay at the concerned faces looking down at her: Mrs Hamilton, the waiter, a bald man with tortoiseshell-framed glasses, a slim girl with short, dark hair and almost identical glasses, and the beautiful lady – now clearly not her mother.

"Oh, I'm so sorry! I-I didn't mean, I mean, oh dear!" Tears stung Jenny's eyes. I mustn't cry! I *mustn't!* she thought, closing her eyes tightly.

"It's my fault entirely, so stupid of me," she heard Mrs Hamilton saying. "We've just come over from Lundy, you see, and Jenny was terribly ill on the boat. She hasn't had anything to eat since six o'clock this morning, poor thing."

"Would my Coca Cola help? I haven't drunk from it," said the girl.

She sounded nice, and so did the suggestion of a Coke. Jenny felt parched, with a peculiar metallic taste in her mouth. She opened her eyes and smiled at the girl crouched by her side, holding a glass of cool, sweet Coke.

The girl smiled back. She had a brace over her teeth, and spoke with a slight lisp. "Hello. I'm Frances," she said. "Are you starting at St Anne's, too?"

Frances' parents introduced themselves as John and Jessica Knighton.

"My goodness! Aren't you our new MP?" Mrs Hamilton exclaimed. "I'm afraid so," Mr Knighton replied, smiling. He asked Mrs Hamilton and Jenny to join his family for lunch, and offered them a lift to St Anne's afterwards.

By the time they were ready to leave the hotel, Mrs Hamilton had told John Knighton exactly what she'd do if she were Prime Minister. Jenny and Frances had discovered they were the two new girls who had been awarded scholarships. What's more, they both played the piano, loved singing and hoped to be picked for the school choir. In many ways, though, they were complete opposites. Frances had been born and raised in London where, it seemed, every minute of her time had been filled with organised activities like dance, drama, music and extra coaching for the scholarship exam. Her idea of fun was a trip to a museum or the theatre. She'd never been near a pony, and she didn't want riding lessons.

Oh well, Jenny thought as she settled into the beige leather seats of the Knightons' black Bentley, at least I've made one friend. I'm bound to find some girls who like horses, and I'll make friends with them too. Perhaps I'll end up with lots of friends!

The car purred down the road. Jenny felt like royalty as they passed along the bustling quayside.

A familiar figure puffed on his pipe and talked to some men mending lobster pots. They all looked up at the Bentley as it passed.

"Coo-ee! Captain Dover!" Jenny shouted, rubbing at the misty window and waving frantically.

He took his pipe out of his mouth, smiled and held his hand up in a brief greeting before turning back to his friends.

"Jenny! Behave yourself!" Mrs Hamilton scolded.

For the first time Jenny felt completely trapped in her new, strange life, like a goldfish in a bowl, looking out at the real world. She longed to be with the fishermen on the quay.

The car turned smoothly over the bridge and then accelerated along a broad road. Jenny flinched every time traffic passed in the opposite direction, expecting a crash. She wasn't used to cars.

Unfamiliar trees, hedges and fields whizzed by. The adults chatted politely, but the two girls fell silent.

St Anne's School for Girls stood, solid and imposing, at the top of a long drive flanked by parkland. Huge trees dotted the lush pasture, which was enclosed by wrought iron fencing. Jenny looked out for ponies, but all she could see were brown cattle and a few sheep.

The two fields nearest the house had goal nets in them.

"Oh, no! Hockey pitches!" Frances groaned.

"What's so awful about hockey?" Jenny asked.

"It's a terrible form of torture invented by sadistic games teachers."

"Nonsense!" Mrs Hamilton said. "It's a great game! I used to love it when I was a girl; I was even team captain for a couple of years. Being in a team is such a good way to make friends, I always think."

They parked next to a row of cars, all shiny and expensive-looking.

Several confident, well-dressed parents stood talking while their immaculate daughters chatted and laughed together. Other families greeted each other as they carried suitcases, trunks and hockey sticks in various directions with the certainty of soldier ants.

Jenny studied the daunting scene from the sanctuary of the Bentley. The new girls are supposed to arrive early, but everyone here seems to know each other already, she thought. Everyone seems to know what to do and where to go. They don't seem "new" at all. This is much worse than I'd imagined!

Mrs Hamilton turned round in her front seat, and beamed at Jenny and Frances. "Here we are, girls! Isn't this exciting?"

13

The noise was the worst thing, Jenny decided after a few days at St Anne's. Worse than having every minute of your day organised, and worse than having to hide in the loo for a few moments of solitude.

The day started with First Bell at a quarter-to-seven. This woke Jenny with the ferocity of a hurricane, smashing through precious dreams of home or blissful, oblivious sleep. Second Bell followed five minutes later, just as Jenny's heart rate was approaching normal again. Everyone then had twenty minutes to wash in freezing-cold water, queue for the loo, get dressed, make beds and tidy up before Breakfast Bell rang. That was just the beginning. The whole day was governed by bells for lessons, breaks, meals, games sessions and even Last Bell for lights-out. Between the bells, noise was supplied by people chattering, talking, shouting, scolding, lecturing, laughing and screaming. The noise didn't even stop after dark. Jenny's dormitory – "dorm" in school language – had nine other girls in it, and they all talked for ages after lights-out. Susie, the Dorm Prefect, was supposed to stop them, but she was the worst offender with her incessant talk about boys. Jenny took to sleeping with tissues stuffed in her ears.

As she'd thought, most of the new girls already knew each other. They'd moved on to St Anne's together from a school called Norwood House, and they guarded their friendships jealously. Within a few days the Third Form had developed an insecure pecking order, with the popular set at the top and assorted misfits at the bottom. Anyone trying to work their way up was very careful to avoid contact with people obviously less popular than themselves, for fear of demotion.

This system, with its merciless unwritten rules and rituals, seemed totally normal to the other girls. Jenny couldn't understand it at all. It seemed that skill at games, good looks and loud self-confidence earned lots of popularity points. Academic ability, shyness and physical imperfections sent you plummeting down the league table. Being a nice person didn't count at all.

Jenny and Frances were labelled swots for winning

the scholarships, and found themselves at the bottom of the pile, along with spotty Alison, shy Pandora, asthmatic Dorothy, nervous Jane and fat Belinda. They became an unlikely group of friends, united in adversity. Frances soon became known as Fran, and some other girls acquired less flattering nicknames. Jenny was glad nobody gave her a nickname. She'd always been Jenny, as in Jenny's Cove.

To her disappointment, none of her new friends liked riding. It appeared to be a hobby exclusively enjoyed by popular girls, who talked enthusiastically about riding, the Pony Club, competitions and anything to do with horses and ponies. Jenny hovered around them, like a moth attracted to a light, drawn by the conversation and longing to join in.

It was during one of her eavesdropping sessions that she discovered there would be no riding lessons until after half term, because the horses at Home Farm Equestrian Centre had equine influenza. Some of the girls had horses stabled there during term time, so they were especially worried.

Dejected, Jenny walked away. She hadn't realised horses could get flu. Her twin goals of learning to ride and rescuing Midnight seemed further away than ever. She had no idea how she'd *find* Midnight, let alone get him a good home! Her best bet was to make friends with some of the horsey girls – but how?

Mrs Hamilton's no-nonsense voice popped into her head: "Being in a team is such a good way to make friends, I always think." Jenny wondered whether it was true. At the very least, it seemed worth a try.

Unlike Fran, Jenny enjoyed playing hockey. The hockey pitches had tremendous views over some fields to the sea, and on clear days the outline of Lundy could be seen, a greyish shape on the horizon, as unreachable as a distant star. The sight of it made Jenny ache with homesickness, but the thought that Lundy was watching over her made her try even harder to play well.

Saturday afternoons at St Anne's were devoted to matches. Girls picked for teams played visiting schools, or escaped on coach journeys to play an away-match. On Thursday afternoons the lists were put up, showing the teams for the following Saturday. If you were picked, you'd made it. Popularity was assured, as long as you didn't let everyone else down. Team members had a special Match Tea afterwards, which was always good because the competition between schools to produce the best tea was almost as fierce as the competition to win matches.

If you weren't picked for a team you were a nobody, and you certainly didn't get any Match Tea. Even the teachers didn't seem to care what you did as long as you signed the Out of Grounds Book and had at least one other pupil for company if you went for a walk outside the school grounds.

On the third Thursday of term, Jenny suddenly became popular.

"Well done, Jenny! You're centre-back. Welcome to the team!" said Lucinda, the goddess-like Team Captain, emerging from the scrum around the notice board.

Other girls crowded around Jenny, offering congratulations and instant friendship. She'd made it!

At supper that night she sat with her new friends. It was an effort to keep up with their self-assured chatter, but thrilling to hear all about Pony Club, gymkhanas, jumping teams and all the things she'd only ever read about before. She was happy just to sit and listen, which was lucky because nobody seemed to be particularly interested in anything she had to say. She avoided looking at the corner table where her old friends sat, and at the empty place they'd been saving for her.

The match on Saturday was an away-match at a school called The Grange. Jenny climbed onto the coach, and slid into a double seat halfway down while the other girls noisily bagged seats and shouted for their best friends to join them. Not for the first time, Jenny felt alone and insecure amongst the fickle, exciting gang she now called her friends. She missed thoughtful, dependable Fran more than she cared to admit.

The seats were covered with a material like thin carpet, which felt rough against her bare legs, and the coach smelled of stale cigarette smoke. It reminded Jenny of the Tavern after a good party. She smiled. In her Sunday letter home she'd have to tell Dad she now liked stale cigarette smoke because it reminded her of Lundy. He'd think that was hilarious. She was always nagging him to stop smoking.

"What's the joke, then?"

Jenny jumped, woken from her daydream. "What?"

Lucinda stood in the narrow aisle by Jenny's seat, resplendent in her Team Captain's uniform. "Something must be funny. You're grinning like a Cheshire cat." Before Jenny could attempt an explanation, she said, "Budge up. I usually sit with Wizzy, but she's not around at the moment, so I'd better sit with you."

Flustered, and deeply honoured, Jenny beamed at Lucinda and obligingly budged up, squashing herself against the cold window and leaving at least three-quarters of the seat free.

"Who's Wizzy?" Jenny asked, trying to find something to talk about.

Lucinda laughed. "You must be the only girl in

North Devon who doesn't know Wizzy! She's in all the Pony Club teams *and* the county hockey team. We always win matches when she's with us.. Everyone loves Wizzy. We're all lost without her."

The coach started with a shudder, and rumbled down the school drive.

"Has she gone to a different school, then?"

"Of course not! Haven't you heard? It was simply *awful!*" Lucinda exclaimed, gripping Jenny's arm. "Her father bought her this new pony. Apparently someone said it was a fantastic jumper, so he bought it unseen. I suppose he wanted to snap it up before anyone else got the chance. Anyway, it turned out to be a *complete* nut-case! She ended up in hospital with a broken arm, a broken collar bone, broken ribs – you name it, she broke it! She's on the mend now, thank goodness, but it looks as if she won't come back to school until after half term. Poor old Wizzy! It was *such* a disappointment, quite apart from anything else. It's *so* difficult to find a pony to take you up to the next level when you're competitive, isn't it?"

Jenny nodded wisely, hoping that was the correct response. You haven't seen Midnight jumping, she thought. Her heart missed a beat, as it did whenever she dared to think about him.

"Oh well, she'll just have to make do with Creo until she finds something better," said Lucinda. Then she knelt on her seat and joined in an animated conversation with the girls in the seats behind.

The bus turned out of the school drive, and they entered the outside world.

Lucinda ignored Jenny for the rest of the trip, apart from pointing at a large house on top of a hill and saying, "Look! There's Wizzy's house!"

Jenny spent most of the time gazing out of the window, trying to remember where she'd heard of a pony called Creo. The name rang a bell, but she couldn't think why.

14

Dear Dad

I hope you are well. I am very well.

I played centre-back in a match against The Grange yesterday and we won 5-2. It was fun and the tea was delicious. I've made lots of new friends and Miss Munroe says I'm an asset to the hockey team.

I've been chosen for the choir. We have choir practise nearly every day.

We can't do riding at the moment because the horses are ill, so I haven't had a chance to wear the hat and jods you gave me.

How's Meg? Give her a pat from me.

Guess what? I've decided I like the smell of cigarette smoke, because it reminds me of the Tavern and you!

Say hello to everyone from me. Make sure you look after Gale.

Please write.

Love from Jenny

Jenny folded her obligatory Sunday letter home, put it into an envelope and addressed it, being careful not to stick the flap down because letters home had to be inspected by Miss Nash. Then she wrote to Mrs Hamilton, giving a goal-by-goal account of the victorious hockey match.

Most of the girls wrote at least six letters every Sunday, and received a steady stream of replies throughout the week. Jenny had received two letters in three weeks: one from her father and one from Mrs Hamilton. More than anything she longed for a letter from Ben, but she was too shy to make the first move and write to him. Besides, she didn't know his address.

Miss Nash was Jenny's Housemistress. She was also the teacher in charge of the post, and she seemed to relish her powerful position, well aware that the arrival of the post was the highlight of the girls' day. Every morning she made them wait while she carefully placed the final few letters in their alphabetical pigeon-holes in the Great Hall. Then she stood back and watched, eagle-eyed, as the girls swooped in like a flock of gulls squabbling behind a trawler.

On Tuesday there was a letter for Jenny. It was her letter home, with SEE ME written in red ink on the envelope. The envelope was empty. Jenny stood staring at it, bewildered.

"Ooh! Who's been a naughty girl?" Lucinda giggled, looking over Jenny's shoulder.

"Are you all right, Jenny?" Fran asked. "You look as white as a sheet!"

"Look," Jenny said, showing her the envelope. Her hands shook. "Do you think something awful has happened at home?"

"Don't worry. I expect it's just old Nashers being petty. She returned my letter home last week because it had a split infinitive. Can you beat it?"

"I expect I probably can," Jenny said, smiling.

Fran smiled back. It was a genuine, uncomplicated smile from a true friend. It made Jenny feel especially guilty that she'd been avoiding Fran lately in a desperate bid to stay in favour with the popular set. "I really like you, Fran. In fact I like you much more than anyone else in this rotten school." She wanted to say it, but she just thought it. Instead she said, "Are you going to choir practice after lunch?"

"Yes. Are you?"

"Yes. Shall we meet in the changing rooms and go together?"

Fran looked pleased. "Great, see you after lunch, then."

Lucinda was behind them, eavesdropping on their conversation. "Look," she said, "there's Nashers going into her study now."

Fran held her hands up and crossed her fingers. "Good luck."

Lucinda blocked her out, slapped Jenny on the back and said, "Off you go! Take your gas mask."

Jenny held her nose and made a comic face at Lucinda. "Thanks!" She went over to the heavy oak door, and knocked hesitantly.

"Come in!"

She entered Miss Nash's lair, with its rigorously polished wood and neatly ordered bookshelves, clutching her empty envelope.

"Ah, Jennifer. Jennifer Medway," Miss Nash said.

"Um, you wanted to see me." Jenny felt like a fish caught on a hook.

"You wanted to see me, *Miss Nash*, without the 'um', if you please," Miss Nash corrected, obviously enjoying herself. She intended to reel in Jenny slowly.

"You wanted to see me, Miss Nash."

"I did indeed. Come and sit down."

As she neared the desk, Jenny couldn't help wrinkling her nose. Miss Nash was famous for her bad breath. Jenny handed her the envelope.

"Ah, yes. Your letter." With deliberation, Miss Nash pulled out the centre drawer of her large desk and retrieved Jenny's letter home. "Your letter," she repeated, dropping it onto her desk as if it were something rather unpleasant.

"If you think I've been smoking because I told Dad I like the smell of cigarettes, I haven't. The seats on the coach smelled of stale smoke, and it reminded me of the Tavern," Jenny said quickly.

Miss Nash was momentarily thrown off course, but she quickly regained her composure. She looked over the top of her glasses, which seemed permanently lodged between two convenient lumps on her bony nose. "I hope you're not telling me you frequent this den of iniquity on Lundy Island, this Tavern?"

Jenny longed to correct Miss Nash, but she didn't dare. Mr Bonham always insisted that to call Lundy "Lundy Island" was wrong, because the name was derived from *lundi*, meaning puffin, and *ey*, meaning island. She said, "Of course I go to the Tavern. It's the place where everyone on Lundy meets up. We have tremendous parties. I mean, it's like – like a village hall."

"I see," said Miss Nash doubtfully. She grasped

Jenny's letter in her mottled, claw-like hands, handed it back to her and said, "Kindly re-write your letter to your father, making it crystal-clear that you have not taken up smoking."

Jenny wanted to giggle.

"And attend to the other corrections, as I have indicated. Do not use slang in your letters, it is vulgar, and if you do not know how to spell, use your dictionary."

Jenny glanced down at her letter. The words *jods* and *practise* had been circled in red ink.

Miss Nash handed Jenny a piece of paper. Jenny read her spidery writing: *You go to choir practice (noun) to practise (verb) singing.* "Write this out a hundred times and bring it to me in morning break tomorrow," she said.

"Yes, Miss Nash. Can I go now?"

"I am sure you *can* go, but you may not."

"Sorry, Miss Nash. *May* I go now?" Jenny asked with exaggerated politeness.

Miss Nash gave her a look which told her she was dangerously close to being cheeky.

"Please may I go now, Miss Nash?" Jenny said in a respectful voice.

Miss Nash smiled graciously. "You may, Jennifer."

 *

After lunch, Lucinda invited Jenny up to her dorm to show her some photos of her family and their ponies. Jenny went willingly, flattered that Lucinda, the most popular girl in the form, seemed to be choosing her as a special friend. Too late, she remembered about meeting Fran in the changing rooms for choir practice. By the time she got down there, Fran had gone.

Until she'd arrived at St Anne's, Jenny's life had revolved around the rhythms of the seasons, the weather, the farm and boat days on Lundy. Unlike most people, her childhood hadn't been carved up into chunks of school separated by precious slices of holiday. But now she, too, was ruled by this rigid structure. Her longing for home became more acute as half term approached. She counted the weeks, then the days. She thought she'd burst with the effort of waiting.

It's so unfair, she thought as she lay awake on the Tuesday evening before half term. When I wanted time to go slowly at the end of the holidays, it sped by.

Now I want it to fly, but it's crawling along. In fact, I'm sure the clocks are becoming slower every day. She ran through the plans again in her head. At midday on Friday she'd take a taxi, which had been booked already, and catch the boat from Bideford Quay to Lundy. With any luck, the weather would stay good and the sea would be calm, and they'd arrive at around five o'clock, perhaps even sooner. That would give her just enough time, if she ran, to go and see Gale before nightfall. She'd have five whole days and an extra night at home before catching the boat back to the mainland with Mrs Hamilton the following Thursday.

In her last letter, Mrs Hamilton had said she was sorry that Jenny's time on Lundy would be cut short by a few days, but the boat was going in for repairs after that. However, they'd stay in the hotel in Bideford for the remaining three nights of half term, and she was sure they'd be able to find plenty to do until Jenny returned to school on Sunday.

Somehow, I'll have to rescue Midnight from Dobbin's yard in those two precious days, Jenny thought. It'll be my only chance before the Barnstaple horse sales. She hadn't worked out how she'd manage it with Mrs Hamilton in tow, nor how she'd buy Midnight if she found him. There would also be the problem of where to keep him. She'd have to cross those bridges when she came to them. Before that, there was Lundy to look forward to. *Nine whole days without school*, Jenny thought. Her heart raced with excitement. It would be impossible to sleep now.

Time almost stood still on Wednesday. The day eventually gave way to the evening, then another sleepless night.

On Thursday the wind, which had been a light south-westerly all week, backed to a south-easterly direction and increased in strength. The air became much colder.

As she lay in bed that night, listening to the wind rattling the window panes by her bed, Jenny prayed it would die down again. Instead, it seemed to get stronger. Exhausted by her previous sleepless nights, Jenny slept fitfully, tormented by bad dreams and worries.

Matron came into the dorm after First Bell. "Jennifer, Miss Nash would like to see you in her study as soon as possible," she said, looking apologetic.

Jenny knew what it was about. She went with a heavy heart.

Miss Nash was almost kind. "I am sorry, Jennifer, but your boat has been cancelled due to the bad weather. I gather that an easterly wind is particularly perilous when attempting to land on Lundy Island. I am afraid you will have to stay here with me, as you have no relations nearby. I know it must be a disappointment for you, as it is for me, but we will make the best of it, shall we not?"

A great lump lodged in Jenny's throat. She managed to force out a hoarse "Thank you, Miss Nash," and then bolted for the door as hot tears started to fall. She rushed for the loos, locked herself in a cubicle and allowed herself to cry properly. Longing and hopelessness swept her away so completely that she almost forgot why she was crying. "Why does it always happen to me?" a desperate voice inside her wailed. "Why is life so unfair?"

The girls around the breakfast table appeared sympathetic about Jenny's plight, but there was a touch of glee in their voices as they talked about it, in between chatting thoughtlessly about their plans for half term. Jenny didn't feel like eating, or talking, or anything. She was the girl with nowhere to go. She sat silently in her own private hell. There was a tap on her shoulder. Jenny jumped, and looked round. It was Fran.

"I heard about the boat. You can always come and stay with me in London, if you like," she said.

Jenny nearly accepted straight away, but the other girls had stopped talking and were staring at her, eager for her response. She knew that if she stayed with Fran for half term it would mean they were close friends – best friends, even – so her decision would show everyone whether she wanted to remain with the popular crowd or not. Did that really matter, though? After all, she liked Fran much more than any of the others, and her parents were really nice. Staying with them would be much better than staying at school, and London could be fun, for a change. Yes, she'd go with Fran, and to hell with her so-called popular friends. Suddenly, a thought occurred to her: what if the wind dies down soon? The boat might be able to sail tomorrow, or on Sunday, and I'll still be able to go to Lundy for a few days. If I go to London, that'll be it; there'll be no possibility of getting home, even if the weather does improve.

"Thanks, but I'd rather stay here," she said. The moment she'd said it, she realised it had come out all wrong. It sounded so ungrateful and horrible. She should have explained *why* she didn't want to stay with Fran. "You see, it's because—" she started to say, but it was too late. Her words were drowned by the excited chatter of the girls at the table, and Fran was already walking away.

After breakfast, Jenny searched in vain for Fran. Eventually she gave up and went to her dormitory to lie down. She had a splitting headache.

The cars arrived in droves at midday. Jenny watched out of the window, burning with jealousy as girls were whisked away to freedom. She saw Fran's parents arrive in the black Bentley, and remembered how kind they'd been. Fran ran down the steps, hugged her parents in turn, got into the back seat of the car and disappeared down the school drive. I could have been with her, Jenny thought miserably. The weather's not going to change. I'll be stuck here for nine whole days with Nashers! How could I have been so stupid?

The last car drove away. Silence. Jenny flopped onto her bed and closed her eyes. The ordeal of half term at school had begun. She sighed, got up and looked out of the window again. She felt like a princess imprisoned in a wicked witch's castle, except she was a pretty horrible princess. No prince in his right mind would want to save her.

A dark grey car came up the drive and stopped outside the main entrance to the school. It was much smaller and older than the parents' cars which Jenny had seen all day. Perhaps it belonged to the Head Gardener, or the Bursar. Jenny watched as a neatly dressed, tall, slim gentleman with grey hair got out and shut the car door with careful precision. He looked strangely familiar.

It couldn't be. It *was!* "Albert!" Jenny shouted, leaping down the stairs to the Great Hall two-at-a-time. Her prince *had* come! Albert had come to rescue her!

*

"Mr Hamilton told the Coastguards at Hartland that you were stranded at school for half term, and they contacted me straight away to see what could be done," Albert explained as they drove out of the school gates. "As it happens, I'm home this week, so it's all tied in very nicely."

Jenny looked at the PK, and smiled. He was a little bit of Lundy, right there beside her – the next best thing to going home.

He drove with careful precision. His car, though obviously quite old, was as clean and polished as a lighthouse.

"It's funny to think you've got a car," she said. "In fact, it's funny to think you live here at all. I hadn't imagined you anywhere but Lundy."

Albert laughed. "And look at you in your school uniform! What happened to the tomboy I used to know?"

"Oh, she's still here, itching to get out."

The Scoines family's home was a pretty whitewashed cottage with blue window frames and window boxes, just by the sea. Unlike the bare South Light, it was full of trinkets, family photos, intricate model ships made by Albert and elaborate soft furnishings made by Mrs Scoines. Like the South Light, the whole place was clean and tidy, with a proper place for everything.

Mrs Scoines welcomed Jenny with a radiant smile and a motherly hug. She was as short and round as Albert was tall and thin. Jenny could see why Ben had turned out stockier than his father.

"I've given you Eileen's old room, in the attic," Mrs Scoines said. "I hope you like it."

Jenny felt sure she'd like any room in the cosy cottage. Ben had talked about Eileen when they were on Lundy. She was Ben's older sister who'd married and moved to Canada.

"Would you like a cup of tea before I show you to your room?" Mrs Scoines asked. She'd already poured one out. "Milk and sugar? Albert always has it with condensed milk. He says real milk doesn't taste right. He's spent too long in a lighthouse!"

"Ooh, condensed milk would be lovely, thank you."

The sweet, mellow tea tasted wonderful – totally different from the harsh, dark liquid which passed for tea at school. It took Jenny back to that sunny morning at the North Light, the first day she'd met Ben.

As if reading her mind, Ben walked through the door. His face creased into the most wonderful smile. "Jenny!" He walked straight over and hugged her, then stepped back to look at her. "Blimey! You *do* look posh! Guess what? I've got the weekend off, so I'll be able to show you the *real* North Devon. Once we've got you into some proper clothes, that is. We don't want to scare the natives, do we?"

All Jenny's fears that things would be different between them on the mainland vanished.

After tea, Jenny and Ben walked along the cobbled streets and stood watching the tide as it raced out, blown by the wind.

At last Jenny could tell Ben about Midnight. Her words spilled out in an unstoppable torrent, like the water rushing out to sea in front of them. "So you see," she said finally, "Not being able to get to Lundy may be a good thing after all. It's almost as if fate has given me this brilliant opportunity to find Midnight and make sure he gets a good home. You will help me, won't you?"

Ben looked worried. "It's all very well, Jenny, but supposing we do find him in Dobbin's yard. You haven't got any money to buy him with, have you? And supposing Dobbin does give him to you, just to get rid of him, what then? Where will you keep him?"

Jenny looked at the ground. These questions, and many more, had occupied her sleepless nights for many weeks. "I thought perhaps I could offer to work for Dobbin in payment for Midnight. I could handle the ponies on Lundy so they're much tamer for transporting to the mainland. That would save him a lot of time, wouldn't it? It'd be kinder on the ponies, too, because they wouldn't be so frightened. And I could keep Midnight at livery at Home Farm. Some of the girls keep their ponies there so that they can ride them once a week from school. I could learn to ride Midnight."

"Simple!" Ben teased. "Or as posh girls say, *easy-peasy!*"

Jenny punched him. "Don't mock! This is serious!"

Ben raised his arms and pretended to look frightened. "Okay! I surrender! Well, if you're certain about all this, we'll bike to Dobbin's yard tomorrow. It's only about five miles from here."

"I've never ridden a bike before," Jenny said doubtfully. "They're not much use on Lundy, you see."

Ben smiled. "Okay, first I'll teach you to ride a bike, *then* we'll pay Dobbin a visit." He looked at his watch. "Blimey, is that the time? We'd better get back. Uncle Bob's coming to supper."

Jenny giggled. "Bob's your uncle," she said.

"Yes, he is. Why's it so funny?"

"It's something Mrs Hamilton says a lot. I think it means no problem, or *easy-peasy.*"

They both laughed. Jenny had almost forgotten what it felt like to be happy. Now she felt sure everything would turn out all right. Fate had given her this opportunity to rescue Midnight, and she was going to make the most of it. With Ben by her side, how could she fail?

Uncle Bob was Albert's older brother. He was a large, jovial man who looked as if he should be a fisherman, but he actually owned an antiques shop in Bideford. He greeted Jenny like a member of the family, and immediately wanted to know all about school and Lundy. Like the others, he seemed genuinely interested in anything she had to say as they sat round the kitchen table and ate a delicious supper of roast chicken. After the strict divisions between teachers and pupils at school, it was strange to be back in a world where adults treated her like a fellow human being and didn't correct her the whole time.

"So what does a bright young thing like you find to do on Lundy day after day?" Uncle Bob asked.

"Masses of things," Jenny replied. "I have to work in the Hotel some of the time, and I help Dad to look after the farm animals, but otherwise I'm free to do as I like. I spend a lot of time with the ponies, especially now I own one of them. She's called Gale, and she's beautiful."

Uncle Bob chuckled. "You girls, you're all the same! If you're not careful, you'll turn out like Rose, our little sister. You ought to meet her sometime, if you like Lundy ponies. She's obsessed."

"You're telling me! It all started when she bought one for her girls to ride ages ago, didn't it? A lovely little mare called Kestrel, I seem to remember. The children did all sorts of things with her, and she was forever winning prizes," Albert said.

"Anyway, not content with one, she bought another, and another, and now she's gathered together quite a herd of them," Bob added. "She collects ponies like I collect antiques. Come to think of it, most of her ponies *are* antiques! She specialises in buying the old crocks from Barnstaple Market every year, because she feels sorry for them and doesn't want them to go for meat. It's lucky she's got an understanding husband who owns a large chunk of Bodmin Moor, that's all I can say."

I've just had an idea, Jenny thought. If Dobbin won't give me Midnight and insists on taking him to Barnstaple Market, perhaps we can persuade Rose to buy him!

Following a brief lesson in riding a bike – a crash course in more ways than one – Jenny cycled behind Ben, wobbling only occasionally, all the way to Dobbin's yard. The thought that she was going to see Midnight spurred her on.

The yard wasn't at all as Jenny had imagined. She'd

expected dirty stables and abused horses, but Ben parked his bike outside some bright white gates leading to an impressive courtyard, surrounded on three sides by airy looseboxes with newly painted dark green doors and window frames. The whole place looked more like a racing stables than a dealer's yard.

"You're sure we've come to the right place?" Jenny asked, surveying the inquisitive horses which popped their heads over their stable doors, ears pricked and eyes bright. They looked well and happy. None of them looked like Midnight.

"Quite sure." Ben gave Jenny a reassuring pat on the back. "Only the best for Midnight."

An Alsatian dog appeared, barking.

"Duke! Go and lie down!" Dobbin shouted, emerging from a room in the centre of the stable block, which Jenny guessed was the tack room. He saw the visitors, raised a hand in greeting and hurried over. His welcoming smile changed to a frown as he recognised Jenny. "What are you doing here?" he snapped.

"Where's Midnight? I can't see him," Jenny blurted out. It wasn't what she'd meant to say, not straight away like that, but she couldn't help it.

"Lord knows."

I can't have heard him correctly, Jenny thought. "Um, sorry?"

"I said 'Lord knows'," Dobbin repeated slowly, as if talking to an idiot. "I don't know, and I most definitely don't care."

Immobilised with shock, Jenny stared at him. "But, but, where, um, where . . ."

Ben stepped in. "Where's he gone, then? Did you sell him to someone?"

"Too right, I did. To a man with more money than sense. He said he'd heard rumours that a stallion called Midnight had come over to the mainland to be sold, and his daughter had set her heart on having him. Someone told her he was the most brilliant jumping pony, apparently. Well, we all know *that*, don't we?" he said, giving Jenny a sly smile. "Midnight had only been here a few days when the man's groom arrived with a fancy horsebox and took him away, just like that, untried, no questions asked. Wish all my customers were so foolish."

"But, but you must have *told* him Midnight wasn't broken to ride or anything!" Jenny exclaimed.

"If they don't ask, don't tell. First rule of horse trading. Now, with that pearl of wisdom to send you on your way, I'll wish you a safe journey back to Lundy."

"Have you got the address of the person who bought Midnight?" Ben asked.

"Even if I had, I wouldn't give it to you, boy.

Customer confidentiality. I doubt Midnight's there, anyway. Didn't live up to expectations, by all accounts. Put the man's daughter in hospital. Bad news, that pony. He's probably gone to Fremington by now. Best place for him." He turned and walked away.

"Whereabouts in Fremington?" Jenny called after him.

Still walking, he turned his head slightly and said, "Where d'you think?"

"Come on, Jenny. Let's go," Ben said. "Let's go home."

"But why won't he tell us where Midnight is in Fremington?" Jenny protested.

Ben put his arm round her shoulder, as if trying to protect her from the shock of what he was about to tell her. "Because he meant the abattoir in Fremington," he said. "Don't worry, I'm sure it hasn't come to that, though. Come on, we'd better go home."

That night, Jenny couldn't sleep. She lay in bed in her cosy attic room, staring at the sloping ceiling. Fragments of memory, like jigsaw pieces, were slowly linking together in her mind. That girl who visited Lundy at the beginning of the summer holidays was called Isabella – Isabella something beginning with W? Wagstaff! Yes, that's it, Jenny thought. I told her I rode Midnight, which was true. I also told her he could jump well, also true. Unfortunately she put two and two together and thought I rode Midnight while he was jumping. I didn't say I did, but I didn't say I didn't. Does that make me a liar? Jenny turned over, and sank her head onto a fresh, cool part of the pillow, hoping it would help her to think. Isabella said she had a pony, Dinglefoot something, which had won so many prizes that she only kept the firsts. Dinglefoot Creation, that's it. What a silly name for a pony. It did have a nickname too. What was it? Creo! That's right. Oh my goodness! That's what Lucinda said Wizzy's pony was called. Wizzy bought a new jumping pony which hurt her so badly that she ended up in hospital. The name Wizzy could be a sort of mixture of Isabella and Wagstaff, couldn't it? She buried her face in the pillow, completely certain now. Isabella Wagstaff was Wizzy, and she'd bought Midnight because of what Jenny had told her on Lundy. She'd told Wizzy she rode Midnight. She'd told Wizzy he was a fantastic jumper . . .

Jenny turned first one way, then the other. The patchwork quilt slid off the bed and slumped onto the floor. She shivered, and closed her eyes tight. Why had she become so selfish and thoughtless? It was her fault that everything had gone wrong. She'd let Wizzy believe something which wasn't true, just to impress her, and she'd dumped Fran, a real friend, because she wanted to be popular at school. Worst of all, she'd lied to Midnight, but he'd been clever enough to see right through her; she'd seen it in his eye when she'd abandoned him on the Landing Beach.

I am responsible. The words haunted her all night.

16

"Are you all right, Jenny? You look a bit under the weather," Mrs Scoines said at the breakfast table the following morning.

"I'm fine, thanks. I just had a bad dream last night. It kept me awake," Jenny replied.

"Oh dear, I am sorry. Why don't you stay here and take it easy today? You must be exhausted after school. Nothing much goes on round here on a Sunday, unless you'd like to come to church with me, of course.

"Um, if it's okay to borrow your bike again, I'd love to go for another bike ride, Mrs Scoines," Jenny said.

"That's fine. You seem to have taken to cycling like a duck to water. I'll make you some sandwiches. By

161

the way, do call me Ada. It seems silly for you to call me Mrs Scoines when you call Albert by his Christian name."

"Thank you, Ada," Jenny said shyly. On Lundy it seemed natural for her to call everyone by their Christian names, apart from Mr and Mrs Hamilton or Mr and Mrs Bonham, of course. And she didn't call Major Bathurst "Batty" to his face, although most of the adults did. However, after the stuffy formality of school it seemed rude to call any adults by their Christian names, even Albert.

"Okay, where to?" Ben asked as they set off, bumping down the cobbled street which led to the main road.

"St Anne's," Jenny said.

"Why there, of all places?"

"I'll explain when we get there."

It was hard work biking against the wind, which was still blowing strongly from the south-east. Jenny had abandoned any hope of getting to Lundy, especially as Albert had said the weather was unlikely to change for the next couple of days, but she didn't really mind. She had to find Midnight.

They arrived at the school gates. As usual, they were shut. It was odd to be on the outside looking in for a change. In fact, it was odd just being there, especially with Ben. Jenny now had separate parts of her life which wouldn't mix, like oil and water.

"You don't seriously want to go in there, do you?" Ben said, pointing at the school gates.

"No fear! I wanted to start from here because there's a chance, just a chance, we may be able to find Midnight, if he's still alive." As quickly as she could, Jenny told Ben about Isabella Wagstaff's visit to Lundy and why she thought Isabella's father had bought Midnight.

"So how do we find out where this Wizzy person lives? Raid the school records?" Ben asked.

Jenny laughed. "No, I don't think we'll have to do that, thank goodness. You see, Lucinda pointed out Wizzy's house to me on our way to a hockey match against The Grange. If we can retrace the route, I'm sure I'll recognise the house."

"It's worth a try," said Ben. "Where's The Grange?"

"That's the problem. I don't know exactly, but I'll try to remember as we go along. I spent most of the journey looking out of the window because Lucinda was gossiping with the girls in the seat behind us."

"Let's have a sandwich; this could be a long day," said Ben.

One of Jenny's dad's favourite sayings was, "If you think something's going to be difficult it'll take a few minutes, and if you think something's going to be easy it'll take all day."

It turned out to be true. Finding Wizzy's house took about twenty minutes, no problem.

"Bob's your uncle!" Jenny exclaimed as they approached some wrought iron gates set in a curved stone wall. "This is it." She got off her bike, and read the name carved into a large stone slab, "Rockleigh Manor".

A drive flanked by post-and-rail fencing led to an impressive stone-built house. It had been memorable to Jenny because it looked like a grander version of Millcombe, the Bonhams' house on Lundy.

"What now?" asked Ben.

"We go in," said Jenny, trying to sound confident.

"Ladies first," Ben said, bowing with mock gallantry.

Jenny's confidence gradually evaporated as they walked up the drive, pushing their bikes. It seemed impossible that Midnight would end up somewhere so grand. Her heart raced as she spotted three horses, or possibly a horse and two ponies, grazing in a field to the left of the house. It was difficult to tell what they looked like because they were wearing rugs, but it seemed as if one of them could be Midnight. Please let it be him! she thought. As Jenny and Ben drew near, the horses raised their heads and trotted over to greet the visitors: a dainty chestnut pony, a slightly larger bay horse and a large dapple grey. No Midnight. Jenny felt a fool for imagining that he could have belonged to this elite group of equines.

A tall, thin man wearing a tweed cap, tweed jacket and corduroy trousers stood at the top of the drive. "Can I help you?" he asked.

Jenny could tell by the tone of his voice that he meant, "What are you doing here?"

"Um, we're looking for the stables," she said nervously.

"No stables here, I'm afraid. This is private property," the man said. "If you want a riding stables, try Home Farm. It's about four miles away in that direction." He pointed down the hill.

"No, we don't want to ride," Ben replied. "We're looking for a pony, and we believe he may have been bought by the owner, Mr, Mr . . ."

"Mr Wagstaff," Jenny said. "Yes, we'd like to talk to Mr Wagstaff, please."

"Ah, I'm afraid he's away for a few days; gone abroad with his family for half term, I believe. I'm Mr Wagstaff's groom."

"We're looking for a pony called Midnight. He's a Lundy pony – a stallion, in fact. We thought he might be here," Ben said, straight and to the point.

Jenny held her breath, waiting for the groom's reply.

There was a pause which seemed to last forever, and then he said, "Ah, right." He looked from Ben to Jenny and back again, frowning slightly. "So why are you so interested in Midnight, then?"

"I knew him on Lundy and I'm very fond of him," Jenny said.

The groom gave a dry laugh. "You must be the only person in the world who is! Are we talking about the same pony here? Dun-coloured? With spooky blue eyes?"

"You mean he's here? He's really here?" Jenny asked, not daring to believe it.

The groom seemed unwilling to look at Jenny now. "I shouldn't get too excited. If he is the same pony, I doubt whether he's anything like the one you once knew. He's not right in the head any more. We've persevered with him, even sent him to one of the top trainers in the country for a while, but he just gets worse and worse. I'm afraid he's a dead loss."

Jenny was horrified. "What d'you mean?"

"I mean the boss has told me to get rid of him before he gets back from holiday, and he doesn't care how. I hate shooting horses, but it'll be the best thing for him. I certainly can't sell him to anyone – couldn't even give him away, the state he's in."

"I'll have him if you're giving him away," Jenny said quickly.

There was a shocked silence, then the groom said slowly, "I don't think you know what you're saying. You haven't even seen him yet. He's dangerous. He'd kill you, given half a chance."

"No, he wouldn't. Midnight knows me," Jenny said.

"Sorry, but I really can't give an animal like that to a young girl," the groom said firmly. "It wouldn't be right."

"But you could give him to me, couldn't you?" Ben asked, knowing he looked older than he was.

"I suppose so, if you wanted him."

"Well, I can tell you now that I do, definitely." Ben said. "And I promise I won't blame you if anything goes wrong."

The groom hesitated. "Well, if you really think you can handle him, you're welcome to him. But I'm warning you, he's a devil to look after. He's jumped every fence on this farm. He even jumps out of his stable, so I'm afraid I've kept him locked up this past month. It's no way to keep a pony, but I had no option. The boss would sack me if Creo or the other mare got in foal to him!"

"Can I see Midnight?" Jenny said. Her heart was beating so hard that she could hear it inside her.

"Well, all right, but I can't say I'm proud about the way he is," the groom said, leading the way round the side of the house. "I've done my best to give him bedding, food and water, but it's difficult to do a proper job when he attacks anyone he sees. As the boss says, he's not worth dying for. Nearly killed his daughter, you know."

"Yes, I heard," Jenny said. "But it's okay, he knows me."

"I shouldn't bank on it. Everyone's the enemy, as far as he's concerned," the groom replied.

The stable yard was immaculate. They went in through an archway with a clock above it. Jenny noticed it was twenty-five minutes past eleven. Several stable doors had smart nameplates above them. Peering into one named Creo, Jenny noticed a clean, airy box with straw banked up on the far side. The groom obviously had high standards.

"To be honest, he's been a complete disaster from day one. It's an embarrassment to have a pony like him in a yard like this. The boss usually only buys the best. I can't think what possessed him," the groom was saying to Ben. "You'll need some sort of transport and plenty of help – you won't be able to lead him anywhere, I can tell you that for starters." They'd stopped by a closed double door in the corner of the yard. "Midnight's in here. It's normally used as a foaling box because it's larger than the other stables, but it's still one hell of a mess, I'm afraid. It's impossible to muck it out with him in there, so I just chuck more straw on top every now and then."

Jenny hurried to catch them up. "Oh, do let me see," she said. She reached up and started working the bolt on the top door loose.

"Careful. He'll attack first and ask questions later, and we mustn't let him jump out. Wait, I'll just go and shut the yard gates, to be sure." The groom ran back to the large double gates beneath the archway.

Jenny couldn't wait a moment longer. Promising herself she'd wean Midnight off sugar once they got to know each other again, she reached into her pocket for some sugar lumps she'd saved from the breakfast table. Feeling sick with anticipation, she opened the top door. The stench of stale urine and dung leaked out. She put three sugar lumps onto the palm of her hand, and reached over the bottom door. "Midnight," she called softly. "Hello, old boy. It's me, Jenny. Remem—"

Her words were cut short as Midnight's head snaked out and his body crashed against the door.

She leapt back, knocking into Ben and dropping the sugar lumps. Midnight's yellow teeth snapped shut so close to her head that she could feel the air tremble.

He lunged again, teeth bared, eyes rolling.

Whatever Jenny had expected, it hadn't been this. What on earth had happened to him? He'd gone mad! There wasn't even a flicker of recognition in those sunken, demonic eyes.

"He doesn't know me!" Jenny cried. "Or . . . or perhaps he does! Perhaps he knows *exactly* who I am! I'm the one who betrayed him! No wonder he hates me so much!" She clung to Ben, wailing like a wounded animal.

"Sorry, but I did warn you," she heard the groom say breathlessly as he ran to Midnight's stable and closed the top door again. "I'm afraid he's a lost cause. It really would be the kindest thing to put him out of his misery. You needn't worry, I've got a mate who works in a knackers' yard. He's very good at his job. It's like turning out a light if it's done properly. The pony won't feel a thing."

"No!" Jenny said, pulling herself together. "No, we still want him. Don't we, Ben?"

Ben looked astonished. "Er, I suppose so," he said. "But—"

"But you'll have to give us some time to arrange transport," Jenny said.

"Are you're *sure*?" the groom replied.

Jenny nodded. "Absolutely sure."

"Right, then. I'll be going home at five-thirty. After that everything will be locked up, so you'll have to take him away before then. Okay?"

"Fine," Jenny said. "We'll be back soon, won't we?" She looked at Ben, who seemed immobilised by shock.

"Er, yes. See you later," he said, and they walked out of the yard together.

"You're completely *insane*," Ben said when they

were out of earshot. "What the hell are we going to do now?"

"I think we'd better try Home Farm first," Jenny said. "Come on."

Home Farm Equestrian Centre was a hive of activity. One ride had just come back, and another was preparing to go out. Children and ponies of all shapes and sizes filled the yard.

Jenny instantly loved the place. It looked like a storybook riding school. Please let it be all right, she thought, as she walked hesitantly into the yard with Ben following a few paces behind. Her desperation to help Midnight was the only thing which kept her going. On the way there, Ben had made it perfectly clear he was having nothing more to do with her foolish plans.

"May I help you?" A slim, efficient-looking lady wearing riding clothes approached with a welcoming smile.

"Um, I've heard you have ponies to stay here on, er, livery," Jenny said.

"Yes, we do sometimes. It depends on the pony. What sort of livery do you require?"

Jenny felt foolish. "What are the sorts?"

"Well, there's working livery, part livery or full livery," the lady explained patiently.

"Which is the cheapest?"

"Working livery. We pay for your pony's keep, and you pay for the farrier and any vets bills."

"That sounds ideal," Jenny said.

"And in return," the lady continued, "we use your pony for riding lessons."

"Oh, not so ideal. You see, my pony isn't broken to ride or anything. In fact, he doesn't really like people at all at the moment."

The lady looked thoughtful. "I see," she said slowly. "So you'd like him to come here to be broken in? I'm afraid that's even more expensive than full livery. How old is he?"

Jenny tried to work it out. "I think about twenty-four," she said, looking at the ponies standing in line, ready to go for a ride.

"Ah," said the lady. "That's a bit old for . . ."

"Oh, and I forgot to say, he's a stallion," Jenny said, with a feeling of impending doom. Tears ran down her face. She rubbed her eyes furiously, but they just wouldn't stop. "P-Poor M-Midnight! He h-hates me! It's all my f-fault!" she stammered between sobs. She felt Ben's arm around her shoulder.

"Jill!" the lady called to a girl who was mounting a beautiful bay horse. "Take Emma with you to shut the gates. You'd better go on without me." Then she turned back to Jenny and Ben. "I think we need a mug of tea and a chat, don't you?"

"Y-yes p-please," Jenny said.

It turned out that the efficient-looking lady, who was called Mrs Moat, owned Home Farm with her husband. She was a riding teacher, and he was a farmer.

Mrs Moat came up with an excellent idea: Midnight could be kept in a field away from the riding stables, with a bunch of young steers for company, until Jenny could find somewhere else. The field was bounded by wide ditches filled with water on two sides and tall hedges on the others, so it was highly unlikely that Midnight would jump out. Jenny would have to pay for his share of the hay, which would be taken to the field once a day, but that was all. Mrs Moat stressed that she wouldn't be able to keep a stallion on the farm as a long-term arrangement, so Jenny would have to find Midnight a permanent home, and the sooner the better. The field would be ploughed up in the spring, so Midnight would have to be gone by then.

Although she hardly knew Mrs Moat, Jenny hugged her.

"How will we get him to the field, though?" Ben asked. "Are any livestock transporters open on a Sunday?"

Mrs Moat smiled. "Well, this one is," she said,

picking up some keys from a bowl on the kitchen table. "Come on, let's go before I change my mind."

To Jenny's relief, the groom was still there when they got to Rockleigh Manor. Mrs Moat backed her horse lorry expertly into the stable yard, and the groom shut the double gates behind them. They lowered the lorry ramp onto the ground just in front of Midnight's stable. The groom armed them all with pitch forks "just in case", and they stood on each side of the lorry ramp while he opened the stable doors and stood back.

Nothing happened.

"It'll take him a bit of time to pluck up the courage to come out," said Mrs Moat. She stepped back a few paces, leaving more room.

Ben and Jenny copied her, although Jenny thought: you don't know Midnight. He never lacks courage. But she was the one who no longer knew him.

Midnight emerged, one trembling step at a time. Dried dung stuck to his body, partially hiding several scars and patches of raw skin. He caught sight of the groom and froze, shaking all over. Then he jumped onto the lorry ramp, missed his footing, went down on his knees, scrambled up again, tripped, nearly went down again and somehow staggered the rest of the way in.

Swiftly, but calmly, Mrs Moat lifted the lorry ramp and bolted it shut. "There's one terrified pony," she said.

The groom looked embarrassed. He walked away to open the gates to the yard.

The lorry rocked on its springs as Midnight began to panic in his new prison. "Get in quickly before he wrecks my vehicle," said Mrs Moat. As she started it up she added, "The best way to get horses to stand still in a lorry or trailer is to get going. They're so busy concentrating on staying upright that they forget about everything else." She gave a rueful smile as they set off with Midnight crashing around in the back. "Well, that's the theory, anyway."

The field was down on the marshes below Home Farm. It was large and flat, with a patch of rushes at one end. The hedges were high, and the boundary ditches were wide and deep. Ideal.

Mrs Moat drove the lorry into the field, closed the gate and lowered the ramp. A herd of brown-coloured cattle loped up and stood around gawping. Midnight stopped at the top of the ramp, trembling in an agony of indecision.

"Let's just go for a walk down the lane a minute, and leave him to it," said Mrs Moat.

They walked down the lane. The evening sunshine bathed everything in golden light.

"He will be all right, won't he?" Jenny asked anxiously.

"To be honest, I don't know, Jenny. Luckily for me, I've had little experience of horses who've been so traumatised. All I can say is we'll do our best for him."

When they got back to the field, Midnight was grazing next to the cattle.

"Well, that's the first hurdle over with, anyway," said Mrs Moat. "I'll pop you both back home once we've picked up your bikes. It'll soon be dark."

"Thank you so much, Mrs Moat. I don't know what we'd have done without you," Jenny said.

"Oh, I expect you'd have managed somehow," she replied.

I doubt it, Jenny thought. Perhaps our luck's changing, Midnight.

17

Ben had to go back to work on Monday. Jenny accepted Ada's offer of sandwiches and the loan of her bike, and went to see Midnight.

She leaned on the gate, and watched as he relentlessly cropped the grass, making up for the weeks he'd been shut in a stable. At last I don't have to worry about where he is and whether he's being looked after properly, she thought. It was a dream come true, wasn't it? But looking at the broken, timid creature who had once been so magnificent and proud only filled her with immense sadness; there was no joy in being with him if he hated her.

She climbed over the gate. She had all day – all week.

If she spent time with him, and got a little closer every day, perhaps he'd learn to trust her again.

Very slowly, she walked towards him.

He walked away, ears back, tail swishing.

She followed him.

Suddenly he charged: ears flat against his head, teeth bared, body low.

Jenny fled for the gate, jumped over, tripped and lay sprawled in the lane. She hurt all over, but that was nothing compared with the utter despair she felt inside.

It started to rain. Jenny trudged up the lane, pushing the bike. She came to a T-junction, and hesitated. What on earth was she going to do for the rest of the day? The rain poured down. She turned left, towards Home Farm.

Mrs Moat soon put her to work cleaning tack, grooming ponies and mucking out stables. It didn't feel like work, though. A boy called Peter and two girls called Emma and Sophie were holiday helpers too. It was fun.

"Thanks for all your hard work," Mrs Moat said at the end of the day. "If you want to come and help for the rest of the week, I'll pay you with some free riding. That's how it works with the others."

So for the rest of the week Jenny spent most of her time at Home Farm, helping and learning how to ride.

She also made time to go and see Midnight, but she never went into his field.

On Saturdays Ben's work finished at lunch time, so he met Jenny at Home Farm. They biked down to Midnight's field together, and stood looking over the gate.

"He's definitely looking better," Ben said.

"Do you think so? I suppose it's more difficult for me to notice, because I've seen him every day," Jenny replied. "At least the rain we had earlier in the week washed most of the dung out of his coat."

"Sorry I've had to work all week, but it sounds as if you've had a good time at Home Farm," Ben said. "I bet you never thought you'd own Midnight and know how to ride by the end of half term!"

Jenny laughed. "Oh, I'm still a beginner at riding. I can't even canter yet. In fact, the more I learn, the more I realise how little I know. For a start, I had no idea how long it took to break in horses. It's incredible that Midnight used to let me sit on him."

"He trusted you. That was the key," Ben said.

"And he doesn't trust me anymore," Jenny said forlornly.

"You'll get there. Just give it time," said Ben. "Look, would you like to come to the cinema tonight? My treat, as this is your last night of freedom. That James Bond film everyone's been talking about is on."

So Jenny saw her first film. It swept her away into another world, and for a while she forgot to worry about anything, even Midnight.

Albert drove Jenny back to school, and Ben came too. Jenny noticed several girls looking at him as he carried her bag up to the dormitory.

"He's rather nice! Is he your brother?" Susie asked when Ben had left.

"No. He's just a friend," Jenny replied.

"What? Your *boyfriend?*" Susie asked.

"No, just a good friend. It is possible to have a good friend who happens to be a boy, you know."

"Ooh! Temper! I don't believe you. I think he's your boyfriend," Susie insisted.

"Think what you like," said Jenny, sounding much cooler than she felt. In the cinema last night, sitting in the dark close to Ben, the thought had crossed her mind that one day he just might be.

At supper that evening, Jenny went straight to the corner table where Fran, Alison, Pandora, Dorothy, Jane and Belinda were sitting with two other girls. She took a deep breath and tried to remember all the things she wanted to say. "Hi," she said.

"Hello, stranger," said Alison. "What do you want, all of a sudden?"

"I want to say I've been an idiot. No, I've been worse than an idiot." This wasn't what she'd planned to say at all, but she ploughed on. "An idiot wouldn't have realised what she was doing, being an idiot, but I did, and I still did it, and I don't know why, except I suppose I wanted to be popular. I let down my friends, and then I didn't have any friends, so I was even less popular. And I did want to come to London with you Fran, but then I thought what if the wind drops and I'm stranded in London? So I didn't, but I could have because it stayed in the east all weekend, but then I wouldn't have found Midnight in time."

Eight bemused faces looked up at her.

"Am I making any sense at all?" Jenny asked.

"No," they chorused, grinning.

"What I'm *really* trying to say is I'm sorry," Jenny said. "Especially to you, Fran. I've been an idiot . . ."

Fran laughed "Oh, for goodness sake don't start all over again!" She shuffled closer to Belinda. "Look, if we all budge up a bit there'll be room for you here."

Jenny got a chair, and sat down between Fran and Jane. They instantly started chatting about half term. There was no boasting or trying to take over the conversation, as there would have been around the other table. She'd forgotten what good company her real friends were. She could be herself again. No more pretending.

Wizzy sat in Jenny's old place at the "popular table". From the glances in her direction, Jenny could see they were talking about her, and she could also see she wouldn't be welcome at their table any more. The amazing thing was that she didn't care.

The second half of the autumn term passed quickly. With Wizzy back in the hockey team, Jenny was relegated to reserve, and was soon dropped altogether because she put a great deal of effort into playing badly. This meant she managed to avoid Wizzy and Lucinda as much as possible. It also meant she was free to walk down and see Midnight on Saturday afternoons. Fran kept her company so she wouldn't be breaking the Out of Grounds rule of at least two people going for a walk together. Midnight seemed to like Fran, despite the fact she knew nothing about horses. Every week he seemed to become a little bit friendlier, until he was allowing Jenny and Fran to touch him over the gate. But he was still very jumpy. A sudden movement or noise could instantly send him bolting away.

"Oh dear," Jenny said after he'd fled across the field because she'd sneezed. "I'll never get him tame enough at this rate."

"Tame enough for what?" asked Fran.

"To take back to Lundy."

"Why can't he stay here, on the mainland?"

"Mrs Moat says I've got to find somewhere else to keep him before the spring, and I can't think of anywhere. Lundy's the obvious answer. He belongs on Lundy. Besides, I've promised him that if he's good I'll take him back there. If he's really tame and well-behaved I could keep him in St Helen's Field, by our cottage, with Kit for company, perhaps."

"You've got it all worked out, haven't you?"

"Yes. Now all I've got to do is persuade Dad and Mr Bonham when I go home for Christmas."

Fran smiled. "Oh. Good luck."

At last it was the end of term. The weather was crisp and calm, and Jenny was aboard the boat to Lundy, wondering whether she was dreaming.

It was too cold to stand out on deck, so she sat on the wooden bench in the cabin. Her body jittered with excitement, but she didn't feel at all sick this time.

"It doesn't seem five minutes since I was bringing you over to start school," Captain Dover said, puffing on his pipe.

"Really? It seems a lifetime ago to me," Jenny replied.

"Bet you can't wait to see your dad."

Jenny's heart skipped at the thought of him. "Yes,

can't wait," she replied, remembering Dad's letters yet again. They'd become much more frequent and chatty recently, and had mentioned Sheila a lot – far too much for Jenny's liking.

Even Fran hadn't seemed to understand the problem when Jenny had tried to talk to her about it. She'd asked questions like, "Why is Sheila so horrible?"

"She isn't. I used to think she was really nice, but then Dad started liking her," Jenny had replied.

"Can't you like anyone your dad likes, then?"

"No, you don't understand. I don't mean like, I mean *like*. You know, all lovey-dovey hugs and stuff."

"Oh! But that's a good idea isn't it? I mean, your dad must be terribly lonely. You can't expect him to stay by himself forever."

"He isn't by himself! He's got me."

"Yes, but you're here most of the time, and it must be lonely for him without a wife."

"A *wife*!"

"Well, it's a possibility, isn't it? Sometime in the future, I mean."

"No it jolly well isn't!"

"Okay, sorry. Forget it."

But Jenny hadn't been able to forget it, especially when it had become more of a possibility with each letter Dad wrote.

184

Her thoughts were interrupted by Captain Dover. "There she is! There's Lundy," he said, pointing ahead, pipe in hand.

Jenny jumped up and peered through the smoke-stained window. A hazy blue-grey silhouette lay ahead. She rushed out on deck. The cold air sliced into her clothes, but she hardly noticed. Transfixed, she watched as the island gained colour and slowly came into focus, until eventually she could make out each cove and headland. Landmarks stood along the skyline: Tibbett's, the Old Light, the Church, the Castle, the South Light . . . Everything in place, dear and familiar, greeting her like old friends. Last of all, Millcombe came into view as they turned and dropped anchor in the Landing Bay.

The boat slapped and clumped in the light swell, waiting for Dad to manoeuvre the landing boat alongside. The distant star Jenny had gazed at for so long had become real. She was home!

The first change Jenny noticed was that Dad had put on weight. He felt much more solid when he hugged her. She had to admit it suited him. His gaunt, haunted look had vanished. And he smelled clean, as if he'd been using some sort of perfumed soap.

To Jenny's relief, Sheila wasn't in the cottage. However, it was immaculate, with freshly baked cakes and scones on the table for Dad and Jenny to eat for tea. They sat down together, and talked as they ate. It was just like old times, yet somehow it wasn't. They each had separate lives now. Life had moved on. Oh, it's so lovely to be home, though! Jenny thought as she listened to Dad telling a funny story about Mrs Hamilton's birthday party in the Tavern.

The following day, straight after breakfast, Jenny went to see Gale. Even the herd wasn't quite the same. She kept expecting to see Midnight, but of course he wasn't there, and some of the older mares had gone too, including dear old Rosie.

The new stallion didn't fit in at all. He was a tall, thin, neurotic creature, and he chivvied the mares constantly. They all looked thoroughly fed up.

Only Gale seemed to be as good-natured as ever. She gave her usual high-pitched whinny, and trotted over. Her thick winter coat was a rich creamy colour, but her legs, mane and tail were dark. The rims of her deep blue eyes were highlighted in black, as if she'd skilfully applied makeup.

"You're so beautiful!" Jenny whispered, stroking her. "Midnight will be so proud of you when he sees you again. He doesn't know it yet, but I'm going to bring him home. Dads and their daughters should stick together, eh?"

Gale nuzzled her coat.

On Christmas Eve, even though it was bitterly cold, Jenny's dad asked her to walk to Jenny's Cove with him.

They stood looking out to sea. The glassy surface of the Atlantic Ocean reflected the feeble winter sun, and scarcely rippled where it met the jagged coastline. The dark cliffs, so teeming with life in summer, were bare and silent.

Dad cleared his throat. "Er, Jenny?"

"Yes, Dad?" she said, with an awful feeling she knew what he wanted to say.

"There's something I want to talk to you about, and this seems like a good opportunity."

She suddenly had a brilliant idea of how to change the conversation. "Yes, there's something I want to talk to you about too. Can I go first?"

"Er, okay."

Here goes, now or never, Jenny thought. "You know I can only keep Midnight at Home Farm until the spring?"

Dad nodded.

"Well, I was thinking, he's becoming much more

friendly now, so I was wondering whether, if I can get him to be really tame and good, I could perhaps, you know, bring him back to Lundy?"

Dad hesitated. "I don't know, love. There could be so many problems – the boat trip, for one. And we wouldn't want him with the herd again. He's sired most of the mares we've got left."

"Yes, I've thought about that. I could keep him in St Helen's Field, couldn't I? He's used to living in a field now. *Please, Dad!* Can you ask Mr Bonham for me? Midnight's been through so much, and a lot of it's my fault. I want to put things right, let him live at home for the final few years of his life. He belongs here, like you and I."

Dad put an arm round Jenny's shoulder and drew her close. "I'll see what I can do, okay?"

Jenny turned her head and looked up at him. "Thanks, Dad."

He carried on holding her. "Now, I've got something I want to tell you. I've been seeing a lot of Sheila lately, and we've become very fond of each other . . ."

Jenny had to listen. She wanted to put her hands over her ears and sing a loud song, but she had to listen to her dad telling her he loved Sheila and he wanted to marry her. It made her cringe inside every time he said Sheila's name. When he'd finished she didn't know what to say. She took a deep breath, and the cold air nearly froze her lungs to her ribcage. "But you love Mum!" she blurted out. "How can you love Sheila if you still love Mum?" There, she'd said it.

Dad sighed, and hugged her even tighter. "Oh, Jenny! Love isn't something you can measure like that! I'll always love Mum in a very special way, but I really do love Sheila too, in a different way."

Feeling dangerously close to tears, she broke away. "I-I just don't think it's right," she said, and ran away as fast as she could, over the rough, frosty ground towards home. In her mind she was asking all the things she hadn't been able to ask her dad: "And what about me? Where do I fit in? Will you still love me?"

On Christmas Day everyone on Lundy had a buffet lunch in the Tavern, in front of a roaring, spitting driftwood fire. With freezing temperatures outside, the Tavern was a haven of warmth and good cheer. Jenny spent most of Christmas lunch feeling wretched. Talking to Dad was awkward, and Sheila was difficult to avoid as she bustled about, cheerfully working away while everyone else enjoyed themselves.

As soon as she could, Jenny escaped. The north-easterly wind immediately sucked the Tavern's warmth out of her. She went home for gloves, a hat and an extra coat, and then went to see the ponies. She'd helped her dad feed them hay near the Quarter Wall that morning, so she knew they wouldn't be far away.

The freezing wind had turned the soil to rock, fossilising hoof prints and tractor ruts. Small white specks of ice floated through the air and dusted the barren ground. Summer was a forgotten dream.

Gale was waiting by the gate. Jenny gave her an apple she'd saved as a special Christmas treat, then she wrapped her arms around the pony's furry neck and breathed in the smell of her. Gale was innocent and trusting, unlike Midnight. Humans had always been kind to her, she had no reason to doubt them.

"I'll get it right with you, Gale," Jenny whispered. "I let Midnight down, but I won't let you down." She sighed. "Oh Gale, I love you *so much*! I love Midnight too, of course, but in a different way." She stopped, remembering what her dad had said. "Oh my goodness," she said slowly.

On the way back to her cottage she thought about friendship, loyalty, selfishness, ponies, life and love. There was a lot to think about.

When Jenny got home, Dad was sitting at the kitchen table, drinking a cup of tea. He looked up and forced a smile. "Cup of tea?" he asked.

"Yes please," she said, sitting down beside him.

"Piece of cake?" he asked. In the middle of the table,

untouched, was a Christmas cake which Sheila had made for them.

"No thanks. I'm still full of lunch."

"Good news," said Dad. "I explained the situation about Midnight to Mr Bonham, and he said that as long as Midnight really *has* turned over a new leaf and is completely tame and easy to handle, you can keep him in a field here. He said he wouldn't mind running a few mares with him either, as the present stallion's pretty useless. Unfortunately Mr Wagstaff persuaded him he needed to get some good breeding into the herd, whatever that means. I thought he was Mr Bonham's financial advisor, not his livestock advisor."

Jenny got up and hugged him around his neck. "Thank you! Thank you so much! That's *brilliant!*"

"I think I probably exaggerated how tame Midnight's become. You may have quite a bit of work to do with him before he comes back," Dad said.

"Don't worry, he'll be fine," Jenny said happily. She sat down again. "Now it's my turn, Dad. I'm sorry about what I said yesterday, but it was quite a shock. I mean, to be honest I did sort of expect it, but it was still a shock. You see, I've been thinking. I love Midnight, but I also love Gale, and having Gale doesn't mean I love Midnight any less. They're different, and I love them both in different ways. Love isn't just one cake which has to be sliced up, is it? It's lots of different cakes for different people, or ponies, or whatever you happen to love. I think Sheila's a very nice person, and if I stopped you from marrying her it would be selfish because I'd be making you miserable just because I want things to stay the same, but they're not the same anyway, are they?" She took a deep breath. "Um, I suppose what I'm trying to say is it's okay if you want to marry Sheila."

The traditional Christmas dinner in the dining room of the Hotel that evening turned into an engagement party, which turned into a party in the Tavern. Jenny couldn't remember ever seeing her father so happy.

Jenny tried not to mind when he took Sheila in his arms and kissed her in front of everyone. She tried not to mind when he talked about the three of them being a family. It was hard, but she tried not to mind. She longed for Ben, and Midnight, and Lundy as it had been last summer – that wonderful time before her world had changed forever.

18

Jenny returned to school for the spring term with a suitcase full of Sheila's homemade fudge and other goodies, to the delight of her friends. They all thought she was incredibly lucky that her dad had chosen to marry such a brilliant cook.

It had been hard leaving Lundy, and Dad, and Gale, and even Sheila, but Jenny had to admit that it was lovely to see Fran and her other friends again. There was so much she wanted to talk to them about. She'd been surprisingly lonely during the holidays.

Her top priority for the term was to make Midnight as tame as possible. She almost wished the eleven weeks of term time could be extended. Ten weekly handling sessions on Saturday afternoons would hardly be enough to teach Midnight all he needed to learn. Lack of equipment was another problem. Ben's rope halter had travelled with Midnight to the mainland and was probably hanging up in Dobbin's tack room, or perhaps it had been thrown away. Mrs Moat had been so kind already that Jenny really didn't feel she could ask her for a head collar and lead rope.

The first Saturday was cold and rainy but, even so, Fran insisted she wanted to go with Jenny to see Midnight. They fitted as many layers of clothes as possible under their school macs, signed the Out of Grounds Book and set off.

Leaving the school grounds always felt like an adventure. The contrast between school and the freedom outside its boundaries was so immense that Jenny almost expected to see border guards with fierce dogs at the gates. In a way, it was extraordinary that pupils were allowed to go out for walks in the countryside together, but the headmistress was a great believer in fresh air and exercise.

"Fudge?" asked Jenny, pulling a couple of pieces out of her pocket and handing one to Fran.

"Ooh! Yes, please," Fran said.

The damp grey lanes were deserted as they made their way down to Midnight's field.

"I can't wait to see Midnight again and tell him he's going back to Lundy," Jenny said.

"Horses don't understand complicated things like that, do they?" Fran asked.

"I think they do. Midnight's incredibly clever. He understands much more than you'd think."

"Well, tell him he's got to become a perfect pony in just a few weeks then," Fran said.

"Don't worry, I will."

But Midnight didn't understand, or he wasn't listening, or he didn't want to learn how to become a perfect pony. When the girls entered his field, he charged around with his head held high, snorting loudly and staring goggle-eyed at them, as if they were the most frightening creatures he'd ever seen. He seemed to have forgotten the trust which had gradually built up between them before the holidays.

"You've got to admit he looks impressive," Jenny said to Fran.

"Yes, but we don't want impressive, do we? We want calm and friendly."

"Why are you always so sensible?" Jenny asked. For the umpteenth time, she walked towards Midnight with her hand outstretched. "Come here, there's a good boy. It's me, Jenny. You remember me, don't you?"

Midnight watched suspiciously as Jenny approached. Then, for the umpteenth time, he shied away from her and charged round the field, setting off a stampede of bullocks in his wake.

"We'll never get him tame by the end of March!" Jenny wailed.

"How about trying to lure him with a piece of fudge?" Fran suggested.

"I thought of that, but I don't want to make him all pushy again."

Fran looked thoughtful. "Do you think we're being too pushy?" she asked.

"What d'you mean?"

"Before Christmas we never came into his field. We just stood by the gate and waited for him to come to us. Today, after abandoning him for over a month, we marched into his field, looking like badly stuffed scarecrows, and expected him to welcome us with open arms, or hooves, or whatever ponies have. Look at it from his point of view. We haven't been very polite, have we?"

Jenny laughed. "You're so funny Fran, and you're probably right too. Let's go back to the gate and see what happens, shall we?"

They leaned on the gate, ate fudge and talked, hardly taking any notice of Midnight. In no time at all he approached them. The bullocks formed a line behind him, wary and inquisitive. Eventually Midnight sniffed Jenny's outstretched hand, then licked it, relishing the sweet residue of fudge on her hand.

"One piece won't hurt, but I'm not going to make a habit of it," Jenny said. She offered him a piece of fudge, and he ate it with obvious delight, curling his top lip as he savoured the taste. It reminded Jenny of the first time she'd given him sugar lumps on Lundy. "Right, let's end on a good note," she said. "Blimey! It's getting dark already."

"Yes, I didn't realise what the time was either," said Fran. "We've got to be back at school in half an hour. Come on, let's run!"

It was difficult to run with so many layers of clothes on, and it was uphill all the way to school. They quickly became hot and out of breath. A green car came up behind them, overtook, pulled in and stopped. A fair-haired boy got out, grinning.

"Ben!" Jenny gasped. "What are you doing here?"

"I could ask you the same thing," Ben said.

"We've just been to see Midnight, and we're going to be late," Jenny said breathlessly.

"You'd better hop in, then. I'll drive you to the school gates," Ben said.

Gratefully, Jenny and Fran got into Ben's car. In no time at all they were at the school gates. Jenny only just had time to introduce Fran and tell Ben about their mission to tame Midnight so he could be returned to Lundy. Ben only just had time to tell the girls he'd passed his driving test before Christmas and had bought his own car with money he'd saved.

"Tell you what," Ben said as they waved goodbye. "How about me picking you up from here next Saturday? I could drive you to the field and back, so you'll have more time with Midnight."

"Brilliant! Thanks so much, Ben! See you here at two-thirty next Saturday!" Jenny said. She dug into her pocket, pulled out the remaining fudge and gave it to him. "Taxi fare. It's delicious – Sheila made it." Then she and Fran hurried up the school drive. They arrived just as the Tea Bell rang.

"Phew!" said Fran. "That was close."

True to his word, Ben was waiting at the end of the drive for them the following weekend. "Late Christmas present for you," he said, handing Jenny a brown paper parcel tied up with string.

Jenny knew what it was straight away, but she didn't say anything until she'd opened it. "Wow! A rope halter!" she said. "Thanks so much. It really is just what I need!"

Ben grinned. "I've brought a bucket as well, and some apples. I thought it would be a good way of giving Midnight a treat, and you definitely shouldn't waste that fudge on him."

Jenny laughed. "Funny you should say that," she said, handing him a tin. "A taste of Lundy, just for you. Happy late Christmas."

Ben opened it. "Ooh! Sheila's fudge!"

Every Saturday until half term, Ben met Jenny and Fran outside the school gates, drove them to see Midnight and dropped them back outside the gates again in plenty of time for the Tea Bell. With Ben and Fran to help her, Jenny gradually won back Midnight's confidence. They both seemed to know instinctively how to handle horses, which was odd in a way because neither of them had ever had a riding lesson. But in another way it wasn't odd at all. They were both their own people – calm, straightforward and trustworthy. And they always tried to see things from Midnight's point of view. It was Fran who thought the best way of catching Midnight when he was being difficult would be to walk away from him, so it could be his idea to be caught. It worked. And Ben suggested that it would be better if Jenny didn't hold the rope tightly under Midnight's chin when he was tossing his head around. He said if he were Midnight he'd find that really annoying. Sure enough, when Jenny gave Midnight more rope he behaved perfectly. Jenny herself found that if she asked Midnight to do something and then relaxed as soon as he did it, she didn't have to keep on asking. With leading, for example, he'd follow her after a slight pull on the rope. After that, all she had to do was walk and he'd follow with the rope loose between them. The three of them – four, counting Midnight – made a good team. By half term, they'd made great progress.

19

The Lundy boat was in dry dock for repairs at half
term, so it was arranged that Jenny would stay
with Ben's family again. Although she was sad she
wouldn't be seeing Dad and Gale, she was delighted
that she'd be staying in the cosy little attic room she
almost thought of as her own, with Ben in the bedroom
below. He'd have to work during the week, of course,
but she'd be able to help out at Home Farm and see
Midnight.

As they all stood waiting for the cars to pick them
up for half term, Lucinda prodded Jenny in the back.
"There's lover-boy, over there," she said, pointing to
the far end of the courtyard.

Ben was waiting in his car, probably too embarrassed to confront the hoard of girls on the school steps. Jenny hoped he hadn't been waiting long. Albert was working on Lundy, so Ben was fetching her in his lunch break.

"Don't think we haven't seen you," Lucinda said. "We know all about your cosy little get-togethers on Saturday afternoons."

Jenny felt her cheeks burning and her pulse racing as she stared at Lucinda, horrified.

"Ooh! It must be true!" she taunted.

Jenny ran to Ben's car, with Lucinda's rasping laugh ringing in her ears.

On Saturday morning, Ben had to work until lunch time, so Jenny borrowed Ada's bike and cycled over to Home Farm. She wanted to tell Mrs Moat about her plans to take Midnight back to Lundy. Mrs Moat was concerned about how Midnight would cope with the boat trip, but even so she offered to transport Midnight from his field to the boat in her lorry.

"Preparation is the key," she said. "I'll tell you what, if young Ben can help you tomorrow, I'll park the lorry in the field for the day so you can lead Midnight in and out. Groom him and feed him in there, and he'll start to think it's a nice place to be. I'll give you some pony nuts and a bucket, and you can play around with him.

I've got an old strip of canvas somewhere which you can have too, so you can pretend it's the sling they have to put around the ponies to get them on and off the boat. Perhaps later in the week a few of us can come down and be "rent-a-crowd". He must get used to having several people around him. There are lots of things he should be prepared for."

Jenny sighed. "I know. It's all pretty daunting."

Mrs Moat smiled. "But on the plus side, he's become so much more friendly and confident in the past couple of months. It has to be down to you, because my husband just chucks some hay over the gate every day. If anyone can get that pony back to Lundy, you can."

Jenny beamed at her. "Thanks for being so brilliant about everything. I'll try to repay you in any way I can."

"I was hoping you'd say that," Mrs Moat said. "Here's a dung fork, the wheelbarrow's over there and the muck heap hasn't moved since you last saw it."

The rest of half term was spent training Midnight and helping at Home Farm, with a bit of time in the evenings for other things, like eating fish and chips on the sea front or going to the cinema with Ben. The days were never long enough. All too soon it was Sunday afternoon, and time to return to school.

Jenny started to worry about Lucinda again. Should she tell Ben not to meet her and Fran anymore? Would

Lucinda tell anyone else about it? No, she wouldn't be that mean. She was just playing her usual cat-and-mouse games. Time was too precious to stop Ben's lifts to Midnight's field. There were only four more Saturdays before the boat trip. Sundays were out because they had church in the morning, choir practice in the afternoon and evensong in the evening. No, she wouldn't say anything to Ben. They'd carry on as usual, and hope for the best.

Jenny's hunch that Lucinda wouldn't tell on her seemed to be right. The first Saturday came and went without incident, and the training session went without a hitch. Midnight now led really well and stood still while the canvas strap was wrapped around him.

Everything changed the following Thursday evening.

"Well done for getting back in the team, Jenny," Amelia said as they passed each other by the science labs.

"What? What d'you mean?" Jenny called after her.

"Hockey match, Saturday. Lucinda's sprained her wrist, so they've shuffled the team around," Amelia shouted over her shoulder. "You're in!"

Jenny couldn't believe it. She raced to the notice board. Her name was there! She'd have to play hockey on Saturday rather than going to see Midnight.

"Don't worry," Fran said at supper that night. "I'll go and meet Ben, as usual, and we'll go to see Midnight."

"I'll go with you, if you like," Belinda said to Fran. "Then there'll be two of us in the Out of Grounds Book."

"Well, if you're sure," Jenny said uncertainly. "But don't take any risks with Midnight, will you?"

"Don't worry. We'll be fine."

"All I've got to do is play really badly, so I don't get picked again," Jenny said.

To Jenny's amazement, Wizzy sat beside her on the coach journey to the hockey match. Without Lucinda, she was surprisingly friendly. In fact, all the team seemed to be much more relaxed in Lucinda's absence. Jenny did something she'd been wanting to do for a long time: she apologised for giving Wizzy the impression that Midnight was broken to ride on Lundy. They talked about him a lot, and agreed that the whole Midnight saga had been one huge mistake. Wizzy said she thought it was really romantic that Jenny wanted to take him back to Lundy. Perhaps it was due to Midnight, but Jenny thought Wizzy had become far less arrogant. It was difficult not to like her now.

The coach journey took ages, and Jenny found

herself describing her training sessions with Ben and Fran on Saturday afternoons.

"Crikey! It's jolly lucky you're here today, because I heard Lucinda telling Nashers there was a prowler in a green car who waited at the end of the drive to pick up girls on Saturday afternoons. I think Lucinda was genuinely concerned about it," Wizzy said.

"No she wasn't!" Jenny exclaimed. "She knows perfectly well it's Ben. She was teasing me about him before half term."

Wizzy smiled. "Well, Lucinda will get into trouble, and it'll serve her right. Nashers will be hiding in the bushes, ready to pounce, and nobody will turn up because you're here. What a laugh!"

Jenny stared at Wizzy, horrified. "No, you don't understand! Fran and Belinda have gone to meet Ben today!"

All through the hockey match her mind was back at school, wondering what had happened. She didn't have to make an effort to play badly.

It was worse than Jenny had imagined. Fran and Belinda were in deep trouble; there was even talk of them getting expelled. And Nashers had reported Ben to the police! Jenny couldn't believe it.

"But didn't you explain about Midnight?" Jenny asked Fran.

"No, of course not. We didn't want to get you in trouble too. You've got to get Midnight back to Lundy. That's the most important thing." Fran seemed remarkably calm about her situation, but Jenny could tell she'd been crying.

"This is ridiculous!" Jenny exclaimed. "You can't all ruin your lives because of me. I'm going to see Nashers right now!"

She knocked on the heavy oak door of Nashers' study.

"Come in!"

Jenny entered Miss Nash's lair, but she didn't feel at all timid this time.

"Ah, Jennifer. And what can I do for you?"

"You can drop all charges against Ben Scoines and let Fran and Belinda off," Jenny said. "I can explain everything. It's entirely my fault."

Miss Nash sat back in her chair, looked disapprovingly over her glasses and said, "Explain away. I'm all ears."

You don't look all ears, Jenny thought, stifling a smile. You look all beak and eyes like a peregrine falcon. She told Miss Nash everything, from Wizzy visiting Lundy to Fran and Jenny's weekly trips with Ben to train Midnight.

The only time Miss Nash interrupted was to correct Jenny for saying that Ben's family were the people she'd stayed with for half term. *"With whom I stayed,"* she said automatically, and then indicated that Jenny should continue.

When Jenny had finished, Miss Nash leaned forwards and said, "Thank you for your very thorough explanation, Jennifer. I appreciate your honesty and your desire to prevent your friends from getting into trouble. *However,* I hope you understand that this misdemeanour cannot be overlooked. Accepting lifts from anyone without the school's knowledge is a very serious matter. The Out of Bounds Book is a system based on trust, and you broke that by accepting a lift in the young man's car. Girls can travel on foot or by bicycle for open air recreation outside the school boundary, but not by car. The rules are perfectly clear."

"I'm truly sorry, Miss Nash, but we didn't realise we were doing anything wrong," Jenny replied. "I haven't seen the rules. Where are they written down?"

There was a pause. "To my knowledge they are not written down anywhere. Until now I assumed they were obvious," Miss Nash said. She cleared her throat. "Very well, it appears that there has been a misunderstanding, and as no harm has been done I will adjust the punishment to fit the crime. You, Frances and Belinda will have a detention next Wednesday after lessons, and we will leave it at that. And I will inform the police that they need not pursue their enquiries. But you are not to accept lifts from *anyone* in future without my prior consent. Do I make myself clear?"

"Yes, Miss Nash."

"You may go now."

"Thank you, Miss Nash." Jenny turned and walked towards the door.

"Oh, and Jennifer?"

"Yes, Miss Nash?"

"Good luck with Midnight. I've always had a soft spot for ponies."

By Sunday lunchtime, Jenny, Fran and Belinda had become school celebrities. Rumours of a handsome fair-haired boyfriend who had his own car and was "at least twenty" circulated like wildfire, along with stories of wild stallion taming on the marshes. It all sounded too thrilling for words!

20

Midnight's return trip to Lundy had been organised to the last detail. The only thing out of everybody's control was the weather. As the end of term approached, Jenny took a keen interest in the wind direction and the appearance of Lundy from the hockey pitches. One of the first rhymes she'd been taught by her mother had been:

> *Lundy high, it will be dry.*
> *Lundy low, it will be snow.*
> *Lundy plain, it will be rain.*
> *Lundy in haze, fine for days.*

It hadn't made much sense when she was living on Lundy, but now it did. Jenny hoped it was accurate, because Lundy looked hazy for a couple of days before the end of term.

On the last night, Jenny hardly slept at all. At a quarter past five in the morning she went to the loo with her radio, tuned it to the BBC Light Programme and listened intently for the final verdict on the weather in store.

" . . . *Lundy, Fastnet, Irish Sea: south or south-west one or two, occasionally three in Irish Sea. Slight. Mainly fair. Moderate or good . . .*"

Better than she'd dared hope for! Now all she had to do was wait, counting the minutes until Albert picked her up at nine o'clock.

She couldn't eat any breakfast. She didn't even want to join in with the end-of-term chatter. The day she'd been longing for had finally arrived. She felt trapped in a bubble of anxiety, suspended in time and place, unable to cope with the magnitude of what lay ahead.

Albert arrived at nine o'clock on the dot. In a daze, Jenny greeted him, loaded her luggage into his car, gave Fran a final farewell hug and settled into the front seat. As they drove away, Jenny felt as if she were playing a part in some film or other. This couldn't really be happening, could it? She couldn't be on her way to take Midnight back to Lundy!

Albert told her about Dad and Sheila moving into Stoneycroft, by the Old Light, and said they seemed very happy there. Jenny knew about the move from her dad's letters. He'd been so enthusiastic about it, saying there'd be much more space inside and a lovely walled garden outside. She wondered whether he'd let Midnight live in Lighthouse Field, next to Stoneycroft. It was a far better field than St Helen's, where she'd been planning to put him. First I've got to get Midnight back to Lundy, then I'll start worrying about minor details like where I'm going to keep him, she thought.

Albert gave Jenny other news from Lundy. Gale and Kit were fine. Lambing had just begun, Batty's birthday party in the Tavern at the end of March had been a grand occasion, as usual, and Mrs Hamilton had excelled herself with a birthday cake which looked like Tibbett's, complete with rather off-putting granite icing which she'd made by mixing burnt toast crumbs with icing sugar. There had been yet another landslip onto the Beach Road, and the first puffins and shearwaters had arrived . . .

Jenny wanted to listen, but she was too distracted to take in what he was saying. By the tone of Albert's voice, he was asking her a question. She tried to concentrate. "Sorry, what did you say?"

"Do you read newspapers at school?"

What an odd thing to ask, Jenny thought. "No. They have them in the library, I think, but hardly anyone reads them."

"Ah, so you haven't seen any articles about Midnight?"

"No. What articles?"

"Somehow they got hold of the story about Midnight going back to Lundy. The upshot is that Midnight's become quite a celebrity, and I'm afraid there may be several people down on the quay to see him loaded onto the boat. Sorry, but I thought I'd better warn you."

"Oh," Jenny said. What else could she say? Nothing, she thought, can make me more nervous than I am right now. I wish Ben could be here! I expect his boss wouldn't give him the day off.

Albert was right. People thronged the quayside, including a couple of policemen and several reporters with large cameras.

He parked the car, and turned to Jenny. "Are you okay? You needn't do this if you don't want to. We could find a home for Midnight on the mainland, I'm sure."

Jenny thought about her dream; the vision she'd played over in her head so many times it had to come true; the vision of Midnight set free on Lundy. She'd rather die than turn back now. "No, I'm fine. Let's go," she said.

They eased through the crowd to the boat, and put Jenny's cases down on the quayside next to it. She saw Captain Dover carrying the mail sack on board, and tried to catch his attention, but at that moment a large man and an equally large lady hurried towards them. The man looked like a fisherman. Jenny recognised him from somewhere.

"Albert! And how are you, Jenny? Quite a crowd you've mustered, eh? I must introduce you to our little sister. She's a great admirer of your Midnight, you know."

Of course! Jenny thought as she shook the lady's hand. Bob's your uncle! Uncle Bob.

The large lady said that she'd bought two in-foal Lundy mares in the past which had given birth to lovely foals, both by Midnight. The foals had gone on to be brilliant jumping ponies with various people, and she was longing to see the famous Midnight in the flesh. She loved Lundy ponies, and had quite a collection of them, but she'd never been to Lundy. Wasn't it always the way? Places nearby always got overlooked when choosing a destination for a holiday. Mind you, being farmers, they very rarely went anywhere . . .

Jenny smiled and tried to make polite conversation, but she was too nervous to think straight. She couldn't even remember what the large lady was called, other than the unlikely label of "little sister".

The police called, "Mind your backs, please! Make way!"

The crowd murmured, and shuffled out of the way as Mrs Moat's horse lorry drew up, halting with a shudder and a hiss of brakes.

Overjoyed, Jenny noticed Ben was in the passenger seat. He jumped down from the cab, grinning. "Hello, Jenny. I like the fan club. Most impressive!"

Jenny laughed, and hugged him. Everything would be all right, now that Ben was here. The lorry rocked slightly, and there was a banging noise as Midnight pawed at the partition. Mrs Moat and Ben went round to lower the ramp.

Jenny had never seen Mrs Moat look so rattled. She stood with her hand on the catch of the closed ramp. "I really think we ought to give up this idea altogether," she said earnestly. Her voice shook with anxiety. "I've been around horses for long enough to know that this is an accident waiting to happen. It's just not safe, especially with all these people around. If Midnight broke free it could be disastrous. I'll tell you what, he can stay at Home Farm until you find him somewhere to live on the mainland, okay?"

Jenny looked at Mrs Moat, Ben, the lorry with Midnight inside, the boat, the settled grey sky and the calm grey water. Everything had been brought together for this moment. She'd been given the chance of a lifetime. She couldn't throw it away. "Thanks very much for the offer, but I really do want to take him back to Lundy. He'll be okay, I know he will," she said.

"I hope you're right," Mrs Moat said, and she and Ben lowered the heavy ramp. The lorry rocked violently. Midnight whinnied loudly from inside.

The crowd became restless with anticipation.

Jenny walked up the ramp, calling Midnight's name. He replied with an affectionate rumble.

Glancing at her audience, Jenny spotted a thin man in a tweed cap. Dobbin!

Midnight pawed at the floor of the lorry, impatient to be released.

Jenny opened up the side-gates, and squeezed through the partition so she could untie him. "There's a good boy. We'll show them what a good pony you are, especially mean old Mr Dobbin out there, eh?" Jenny whispered.

Midnight nuzzled her. He seemed remarkably unruffled, and none the worse for his journey so far.

"We can do it! I know we can," Jenny told him. "I'm taking you back to Lundy, Midnight, just like I promised. You'll be there by lunch time, and you'll never have to leave again." She opened up the partition, and led him to the ramp.

He hesitated, snorting at the scene which greeted him.

"Come on. You'll be fine. Don't take any notice of them. Just follow me," Jenny whispered. Feeling incredibly calm and positive, she led the way down the ramp, giving him plenty of lead rope so he could pick his way down.

After a slight pause, he followed.

The crowd fell silent.

Jenny caught Dobbin's eye, and couldn't help feeling smug. She led Midnight round the side of the lorry to the waiting boat.

He went tense.

"There's a good boy," she whispered, stroking him.

Captain Dover approached, carrying the canvas sling. Midnight grunted and shied away, nearly knocking Jenny over.

"Can I do that?" Jenny said. "It'll be better if I do it."

But it wasn't any better. In fact, every time she tried to get the sling over his body Midnight became worse, until he reared right up in the air.

The crowd gasped.

Jenny heard a man say, "This is more like it." She felt like strangling him. "Please Midnight! Please be a good boy!" she said under her breath. "We've been through so much to get this far. Don't ruin it! Please be good!" In desperation she tried to throw the sling over his back.

Midnight reared again, so high that he nearly fell over backwards, and then plunged forwards, ripping the rope through Jenny's hands.

She hung on valiantly, tears stinging her eyes.

He wheeled round and looked straight at her, trembling.

Frightened, humiliated and dreadfully disappointed, Jenny stared back. Why on earth are you being so stubborn? she thought wildly. Why are you being so horrible, after all I've done for you? Don't you see how important this is? You've got to have this sling on! You've got to!

"Oh, I can't bear to look! He's scared stiff, the poor thing. If only you'd told me about him, Bob! I'd have given him a home like a shot. He'd have been happy as Larry running with my mares on the moor at Highridge, I know he would. What a pity!"

Jenny couldn't place the voice, but she knew she'd heard it before. Perhaps it was a voice in her head, like a sort of déjà vu. She looked at Midnight, and she didn't see a stubborn, naughty pony any more. She saw a terrified pony re-living the most awful experience of his life, and rapidly losing faith in the one person he thought he could trust. She must have been blind! She'd been so absolutely determined to make her dream come true that she hadn't noticed it was turning into Midnight's worst nightmare. He'd been screaming at her, and still she hadn't listened.

"Come on, Bob. Let's go. I can't bear to stay a minute longer," Jenny heard the same voice say.

She looked into the crowd, and saw Uncle Bob and his sister, Rose – Jenny remembered her name now – turning to leave.

"No! Wait!" Jenny shouted. "Please don't go! Did you mean it? Did you mean you'd give Midnight a home, running with your mares on the moor?"

Rose pushed through the crowd and came towards her. "Yes, of course I meant it!" The crowd parted, letting her through. Everyone fell silent, straining to hear the outcome of the drama.

"How much would you want? For livery, I mean? How much will it cost me to keep him with you?" Jenny asked anxiously.

Rose smiled. "Oh, I wouldn't want any money! In fact, if he runs with my mares and gives me some foals, I ought to pay you a stud fee – or we could share the foals, perhaps."

"That sounds fair," said a man standing near Jenny.

"And you'll be welcome to come and see him any time," Rose continued. "It'll be a home for life, free of charge. He'll have acres of moorland to run on with the mares, with some woodland for shelter and a choice of several streams for water. I'll take good care of him, I promise."

By chance, just at the right moment, Midnight pawed at the ground.

"I think that means, *yes, please!*" Jenny said.

21

Mrs Moat, incredibly relieved that disaster had been averted, offered to drive Midnight to Highridge Farm on Bodmin Moor, where Rose and her husband, Harry, lived.

Midnight seemed only too glad to get into the lorry again, away from the boat and the horrible sling. Captain Dover agreed to postpone sailing until the following day. He seemed pretty relieved, too.

Jenny and Ben squashed into the cab of the horse lorry with Mrs Moat. Bob and Rose went on in front, riding in Bob's sports car. Albert went to pick up Ada, so they could join the unexpected party.

The lorry droned and swayed. The cab felt warm. Exhausted, Jenny allowed her eyes to close.

She woke suddenly, slightly embarrassed to find her head resting on Ben's shoulder. "What on earth was that?" she said, sitting up and looking out of the window. "It sounded like thunder!"

Ben laughed. "Don't worry. The lorry's just gone over the cattle grid to Highridge Farm. We've arrived."

Bob, Rose, Harry, Albert and Ada stood waiting for them in the farmyard.

Rose pointed towards a dirt track leading from the yard. "Can you drive up there? It'll be so much easier than leading him all the way, especially if he's a bit excited," she said. "We'll go in front with the Land Rover."

"I'll give it a go," Mrs Moat replied, full of her usual can-do attitude once more.

They drove carefully up the rugged track. The small green fields around the farm rapidly gave way to larger, rougher fields and then open moorland.

It's like a large-scale Lundy, Jenny thought, complete with granite rocks. Midnight will love it! "I'm so glad Bob's your uncle," she said to Ben. "And Rose is your aunt!"

They drove through a gate onto the moorland, and parked on some level ground.

Rose strode away up the hill, and shouted with

incredible force, "Hey-up! Hey-up! Come on, girls! Hey-up!" Then she strode back down again.

Midnight whinnied, and pawed the floor of the lorry.

"I think we'd better let him out," said Mrs Moat.

Although Jenny's hand stung from the rope burn, she insisted on leading Midnight. Sweaty and wide-eyed, he skittered down the ramp, but didn't try to pull away.

"Where are the ponies?" Jenny asked anxiously.

"They're coming," Rose said.

Midnight rubbed his sweaty, itchy head against Jenny's arm. "Don't do that. It hurts," she said mildly, rubbing his neck, secretly glad he still liked her.

His head shot up. Alert and proud, he stared into the distance, and whinnied.

A reply came immediately from over the hill.

He pawed the ground and shook his head with frustration. Trying to make her painful fingers work properly, Jenny undid the buckle of the headcollar and set him free.

To her surprise, he just stood there, as if trying to take in what had happened. His body quivered with excitement.

A pony came galloping over the hill, then another, and another – seven in all.

Midnight whinnied again, and set off with huge, floating strides towards the herd. He made a beeline for a strawberry roan. They greeted each other with squeals of joy.

"I'm sure he knows her," Jenny said, thrilled that Midnight had found a friend so quickly.

"I expect so. I bought that mare at Barnstaple Market last autumn, mainly because of her name," Rose said.

"What is it?" Jenny asked.

"Rosie."

"They were best friends on Lundy! Oh, that's brilliant!" Jenny exclaimed.

The mares wheeled and pranced, all trying to impress Midnight. He looked very impressed. In fact, he looked overjoyed.

As the herd cantered down the hill towards her, Jenny realised this was better than her dream. Here Midnight could be wild and free with his best friend, Rosie, and some other old friends too, by the looks of it. *This was Midnight's dream.*

The ponies came right up to the people gathered by the lorry, skidding and cavorting. One, a pretty mare with amber eyes and a rich golden dun coat, approached Jenny and nuzzled her hand.

Jenny stroked her. "She's beautiful," she said. "Did she come from Lundy as well?"

"Yes," said Rose. "All these mares did, at one time or another. That one's been here several years now, and she's a real sweetheart. Someone on Lundy certainly made an excellent job of taming her. I was given her on condition that she had a good home for life. You arranged it all, didn't you, Albert?" Rose looked at Albert, and then back to Jenny. "Our girls used to ride her a lot when they were here, but now she just runs with the rest of the herd. It's a waste of a good pony, really, and I think she misses all the attention. Perhaps you could take her out sometimes, when you come to visit."

"What's her name?" Jenny asked, knowing in her heart what the answer would be.

"Puffin."

AUTHOR'S NOTE

Many thanks to my husband, Chris, for marrying me, choosing Lundy as our honeymoon destination, providing the illustrations for this story and lots more besides. And thanks to other family members, especially our children and my mum, for all their support.

Horses have always played an important part in our lives, from untamed Exmoor ponies to Shire horses. When our children were growing up they had a part-bred Lundy mare, called Kizzy, who was a brilliant jumper. We were told she'd inherited her talent from a legendary stallion called Midnight.

A quest to find out more about Midnight and

the history of Lundy ponies resulted in many new friendships and, ultimately, led to this story. I'm especially grateful to Diana Keast, Chris Price, Peggy Garvey, Penny and Kate Ogilvie, Bridget Long, Mary Courtenay, Mary Oldham, David Dyke, Jan Symons and Mary Gade and her daughters, Jane and Anne-Marie, for making my research so fascinating and enjoyable.

Elizabeth Bradshaw, Marcia Monbleau, Sally Chapman-Walker and Sue Croft are trusted friends who gave me particularly valuable feedback.

I would also like to thank Fiona Kennedy, Felicity Johnston and the team at Orion for all their help and hard work.

In this story I've tried to reflect the spirit of Lundy in the 1960s while keeping all the characters, including the owner, completely fictional.

All the places on Lundy in the book are real because it's difficult to create imaginary places on such a well-known island, although there have been several changes since the 1960s. The Manor House Hotel has been converted into holiday cottages, for example. However, several locations on the mainland are made up, including St Anne's School, Home Farm, Highridge Farm and Rockleigh Manor.

Midnight is fictional to a certain extent, but some of

the things I found out about the real Midnight were so fascinating that I couldn't resist blending fact with fiction.

The Real Midnight

There have been ponies running free on Lundy ever since 1928, when Martin Coles Harman (Diana Keast's father) brought a herd of forty-one New Forest ponies to Lundy, followed by a Welsh Mountain stallion a couple of years later.

Midnight in this story is fictional, but he's based on a real Lundy pony, called Midnight, who was born on the island in the 1930s and was the dominant stallion from 1945 to 1961. Most of the Lundy ponies alive today are related to him.

Lundy ponies are typically dun-coloured, and Midnight in this story is golden dun. However, the real Midnight was a dark liver chestnut colour, with blonde highlights in his mane and tail and a wide white blaze on his head. He had striking midnight-blue eyes and, by all accounts, was a force to be reckoned with. The lighthouse-keepers called him Boris (after Boris Karloff, the horror film star) because he used to chase them as they walked to the Tavern in the evening.

He was a brilliant jumper. Diana Keast remembers

seeing him jump over walls and slate stiles, roaming where he pleased.

David Dyke, who holidayed on Lundy as a boy, has vivid memories of being cornered by Midnight in the ruins of a cottage, and being rescued by his father, John Dyke.

Midnight hated being handled or stabled. He escaped shipment to the mainland several times by jumping out of the handling pens or, on one occasion, over the shippen wall into Pig's Paradise.

Eventually Midnight was caught in the autumn of 1961, following a spirited fight which left at least one man injured. He was shipped in the *Lundy Gannet* to the mainland and sold to Mr Chugg, who sold him on at Bampton Fair a few weeks later.

A lady called Peggy Garvey heard from a Romany friend that Midnight was going to Bampton, and she was determined to buy him. Poor Midnight was in a very sad state, so she managed to buy him for a knock-down price. He had a good home for the remaining five years of his life, running with Peggy's Lundy mares near Okehampton in Devon. He repaid her kindness by siring several lovely foals, which were all good jumpers, and she started up the Braetor herd of Lundy ponies with his offspring. Her breeding programme on the mainland became vital to the survival of Lundy ponies, because by

1990 there were just three registered mares left on the island. Since then, the number of ponies has increased again.

Peggy has many memories of Midnight, like the way he effortlessly cleared five-bar gates from a trot, and the way he used to evade capture by snatching the headcollar out of her hand and running off to drop it at a safe distance before coming back for the edible bribe in a bucket.

However, her most extraordinary memory is of finding Midnight frozen to the spot, barely alive, after a blizzard in the "Big Freeze" of 1963. She managed to get him back to a warm stable and gently thaw him out. Unfortunately, as he came round he became dangerously agitated, and Peggy had to hide in a hay rack for several hours until her husband came home from work and rescued her!

Midnight never returned to Lundy, but his descendants – and his memory – live on.

An Amazing Coincidence

When I'd finished writing this story I met a lady who's now living on Exmoor, working with horses. She grew up on Lundy in the 1990s, loved the ponies and dreaded leaving them when she had to go to boarding school on the mainland. The stallion on the island at that time was Braetor Lapwing (Midnight's grandson) and she used to ride him in secret without a saddle or bridle. Her name, in case you haven't guessed, is Jenny.

Victoria Eveleigh
North Devon
February 2012